THE BLINDMAN'S HAT

Bernard Cohen was born in 1963. His stories and articles have appeared in newspapers, magazines and literary journals in Australia, New Zealand and the United States. *Tourism*, his first book, was published by Picador in 1992. Bernard Cohen lives in the Blue Mountains outside Sydney, having returned from Europe where he spent six months in residency at the Keesing Studio in Paris granted by the Australia Council.

THE
BLINDMAN'S
HAT

Bernard Cohen

ALLEN & UNWIN

First published in 1997 by
Allen & Unwin
9 Atchison Street
St Leonards NSW 2065
Australia
Phone: (61 2) 9901 4088
Fax: (61 2) 9906 2218
E-mail: frontdesk@allen-unwin.com.au
URL: http://www.allen-unwin.com.au

National Library of Australia
Cataloguing-in-Publication entry:

Cohen, Bernard, 1963– .

    The blindman's hat.
    ISBN 1 86448 316 4.
    I. Title.

A823.3

Set in Palatino and Memorandum by DOCUPRO, Sydney
Printed and bound by Australian Print Group, Maryborough,
Victoria.

10 9 8 7 6 5 4 3 2 1

Acknowledgements

The great majority of this book was written during the course of a 1996 Literature Fund fellowship from the Australia Council, the Commonwealth government's arts funding agency.

Thanks to my sister Tamara Cohen, Simon Gilchrist, and Peter Bishop, Director of Varuna Writers' Centre, Katoomba for their comments on and assistance with elements of the manuscript, and to my editor Sandy Webster for her deeply engaged and utterly objective critique.

Nicola Robinson provided good ideas at the beginning (like 'why don't you make it a crime story?') and detailed comments on each draft of this book. Being around also helped—this book couldn't have been written without her.

For Nicola

CHAPTER 1

A couple of breeders are really going for it. He's a grunter and she's a panter. The whole thing's totally percussive for its entire observable duration. Two millilitres of perspiration percolate to the surface of their skins. All fluids are retained within the closed system—that is, between the sheets. Actually, it is not quite true that the system is self-contained. The top sheet is kicked off halfway through. Little is left to the imagination excepting the question 'Who are they?' It could be me and Dida but I can't tell because the woman on the bed isn't wearing a white hat and my dog Muffy is nowhere in sight.

Muffy (having snuck into the New York Metropolitan Museum of Art, reading off the information card): *The game is carambole, played with one red and two white balls on a table without pockets, but the true subject of the painting is sexual flirtation.*

That's Muffy. Muffy is a dog and my companion in New York. Muffy is quite small. He is covered in white hair. He communicates by licking and by scratching

1

the furniture. Sometimes by barking. Muffy is very intelligent and complex. This makes it hard to know or to guess correctly what it is that Muffy is thinking.

Oh, and I'm Vernon. Hi. I'm the one doing the talking. Most Americans call me Vern. (In Australia, my former country, people were roughly divided among Vernon, Vernsie and mate.) This afternoon, I have a sore neck from watching Muffy chase sparrows in the park. Back and forth for over an hour, like watching tennis in low gravity. Now I'll want to see a physiotherapist or some other quack. I mean, it's so easy to overdo these outdoor activities.

Muffy's life is much simpler than mine is. He knows what he likes and is not beholden to anyone for confirmation of the validity of his tastes and beliefs. Whenever it all becomes too much for one former Australian, I take *un momentito* to commune with my little dawg. Muffy's cute fringe hangs over his deep, enigmatic eyes; his tongue hangs from the left of his mouth then from the right and back to the left again, as if mimicking the swings of intending voters in the weekly opinion polls.

I've been in newspapers for all but three years of my time in New York, and have grown used to their many repetitions. (For legal reasons—as I shall explain—I can't name the particular newspaper I worked for, so I'll refer to it as [Newspaper]. If [Newspaper] were a famous person, I could say whatever I damn well wanted to say about it on the off-chance I'd uncover another Watergate scandal. I'd have the full force of the public figure defence to back me up. But as it's not, I must be more careful about libelling it.)

Muffy, despite his habits and clearly expressed preferences, cannot be gotten used to. He is constantly surprising. He re-acquaints himself with the objects in a room in a different order each day; his level of friendliness to strangers varies according to his mood or their odour; and, although his are most expressive dog's eyes, it is impossible to tell what cerebellar event any given optical twinkle indicates.

Muffy: *New Yorkers and people from Sydney, Australia, differ in subtle yet noticeable ways. They are the same types of people: tall men with spectacles and partings; young women in blue jeans who tread lightly; men who cut themselves shaving and have disproportionately large feet; children in grey woollen sleeveless pullovers; people with the initials RW sewn into their handkerchiefs; people on the post-office steps, reading; people with big hair; boys dressed entirely in green; people carrying bags in the crooks of their arms; muscular youths on bicycles; short girls tying shoelaces; stationary people with pursed lips; people wearing new jackets to test the windproofing; others.*

The difference is in the development of the facial musculature. The difference is in the shape of the legs. In both places, people are like elongated dogs, only friendlier.

Muffy and I walk through Central Park. There is a woman in a white sunhat. I am drawn toward her by the intricate machinations of fate. There she is beside the path in the park's 'quiet area', a half-eaten chocolate bar by her side, singing along with her portable radio. Three or four mobile phones are scattered on the ground around her, and she is attacking another with a screwdriver. Could this be the art for which I have been searching? No, I discover later: it is another lost career.

I call out, 'Hey! Hi!'

Muffy barks.

She waves but doesn't move and I go over to her.

3

She clips the back half to the front half of a mobile, and adeptly joins them with a screw.

'Hello,' she says to Muffy.

'This is Muffy,' I say. Muffy licks her shoe.

'Hi Muffy,' she says. 'I'm Dida.'

'I'm Vernon,' I intercede. 'You want me to buy you an ice cream, Dida?'

'Sure,' she says, gathering the phones into a brown attaché case. 'That would be nice.'

Nice. This is how people are met in New York. I go to a nearby ice-cream stand and buy two cones.

Dida and I eat ice creams. We talk about dogs, weather, the newspaper business in which I am implicated as senior sub-editor. I drop bits of cone to Muffy. When we finish eating, Muffy starts to whine.

'Once something is established, it must continue for eternity, or Muffy will be disappointed,' I explain.

Dida pats Muffy on the head. Muffy licks her hand.

'Can I meet you tomorrow?' she asks, and for a moment I think she is talking to the dog, so she has to clear her throat at me before I respond.

'Yes. I would like to do that,' I tell her.

When Dida stands up again, Muffy barks. In the distance, some other dogs bark too.

That night, Muffy and I are sitting in the kitchen. Dida could be sitting in a kitchen too, for all I know. I'm waiting for the water to boil and Muffy's waiting for a biscuit. For all I know, some guy in a chequered shirt could be waiting for a biscuit too.

Muffy: *Who owns the rail lines on which we run our trains? Who owns the roads and the bridges and the fields and the rows of apartment buildings and the footpaths and the ventilator columns and the skyscrapers and the under- ground streams and the window frames and the bookshops and streetlamps and hoses and who has rights over the guttering and fencing and doorways and who holds leases for the wharves and bar-room pool tables and the clocktowers? Who in the end will retain our waste products and our oil paintings and the shoes we place on feet? Who decides the fates of the printing presses and the cable cars and the illumination of national monuments and who determines the distribution of gold and petrol and clothing and glass and chocolate and paper and milk? Who is the proprietor of the wires stretched above the streets and of the articulated lorries and the trash cans on posts?*

I think the answer is Dog.

I am pacing. I'm seeing Dida at 4 p.m. tomorrow in a café in SoHo. It is too many hours from now. I wish I had something interesting to stare at. I wish I had something else to think about. I waste time retracing steps in my mind: where was I on the morning of the twelfth at 11.20 a.m.? If I had neglected to leave Sydney all those years ago, would I be happier now? Not constructive. Stop that. Instead, I map out alternative meanings for facial expressions. The ice-cream seller wasn't bored stupid, he was remembering the face of 'Texas' Harado, backslammed onto the mat by Big Joe Atlas to end the bout after only twenty-five seconds. That little girl on the bus was surely thinking about the steam hovering above the vents on Avenue of the Americas at 33rd: does it taste? how quickly can it absorb the sugary scent of a nearby candy store? I contemplate the possible outcomes of our first date. In some scenarios, we are both happy. In others, Dida is happy and I am not: she walks carelessly away.

I had suggested to Dida that we meet in a particular café with a courtyard so Muffy can be restrained in safety rather than facing mistreatment or over-enthusiastic attentiveness from passers-by. Dida laughed. I wondered what was so funny. My poor little dog, who everyone thinks is absolutely too cute. Later that night, I fall asleep for a few hours. I wake up the next day and I still have not yet met with Dida in the café.

Oh, and the meeting goes off fine. Oh, and afterwards we kiss real tentatively, our lips only slightly moist. Oh, and yeah, it would be great to see you again. Oh, in about an hour? Oh, OK, sure, OK, after dinner then. Oh. Oh OK, for coffee tomorrow morning (breakfast?). Oh, I know you're not trying to put me off too much. Oh, yeah, I think I can wait about fourteen hours too.

Muffy, on the other hand, is incapable of waiting for anything. Now, now, now, he barks into the dusty afternoon.

During our next meeting, Dida and I spend the morning in bed with each other.

I say to her, 'I want you to make me feel really good,' and she replies, 'That's what I want from you too.'

I like sex so much that over the next few weeks I completely forget the career path I had mapped out. I neglect to attend my place of employment at all. The first few days, I think to myself, Well, you really ought to get up and go to work now, Vernon. I lie on my back and smile at the ceiling while I think this thought. Down on the streets, no doubt, copies of [Newspaper] continue to appear on newsstands, the process completely independent of my participation. Some time, I must telephone and apologise for not making it to the office. This is an easily and endlessly deferrable intention, especially because when my colleagues ask me why I'm not showing up, my total explanation can only be in the words of Bartleby: 'I'd prefer not to.'

It quickly seems natural not to work. I wonder how I kept at it for so long. Through Dida I have rediscovered the leisure of youth and it is very good. In my new and plentiful spare time, I imagine Dida's life story.

- She's a poor orphan and I save her. I find her outside a supermarket and I take her inside: that's how a person shows compassion for those less fortunate. She's very grateful. We get to know each other slowly. When circumstances are about to separate us—time to move on, having taught each other so much, nearly everything— we each realise we're in love . . . but how to tell the other, how to take the risk of speaking . . . ???

- I'm a trapped careernik and *she* saves *me*, exposing to me my inner depth and the greatness of humanity. I give up all things cheap and tacky for the spiritual, but she has her calling and moves on, both of us sadder and yet happier for the experience.

- She's a part-time bank clerk who was in the Marine Reserves at Penn State, and at one time held the on-campus record for M16 reassemblage—a record only broken in 1992 by a visiting ex-Green Beret on the college talks circuit.

- She's a failed off-Broadway actor who quit after a decade as stagehand. The other day I thought I saw her trying to learn Teiresias's lines from *Oedipus Rex*: 'When you can prove me wrong, then call me blind.'

Confronted with this, she claimed she was calling her credit provider about an overcharge and had said, 'When you can prove me wrong, call me back.'

- Her Honours thesis concerned disturbed sleep patterns in canines and vulpines. This is why Muffy feels so relaxed around her and why I am on occasion jealous of their relationship.
- She's a former porn star who appeared in *Pulsing Lips* and several other classics of the blue screen. She's still famed for her genital toning, sometimes stopped in the street by women for tips, stared at by men, once approached by a man to sign his condom wrapper, and now usually wears dark glasses out.
- She's a successful architect, though recognised only by peers, not the general public. Her wind-harnessing designs have revolutionised the city's approach to air movement.

  'Warm spaces need not suffocate,' she is quoted as saying in a recent *New York Architecture Review*. 'I want my designs to create cascades of warm air through the New York winter.'
- She's not yet ready to settle down to a career or to dedicate herself to one path. Vocationally, she still wants to play the field, to gain as wide a variety of experiences as possible.
- She works for a rival newspaper, and has entrapped me. Or, she works for a rival newspaper, and I have entrapped her. The newspaper game is a tough world and you shouldn't expect the other guy to go easy. You shouldn't want it, either. It's what makes journalism so exciting: the competition for new stories, new angles on old stories, famous people telling old angles on old stories.

What Dida would say to all this: 'Puh-leease!'
She admits to being a graduate in telecommunications

engineering. I know no one technical. It is impossible that I should be compatible with an engineer.

'Engineering graduate,' she corrects. 'A former engineer.'

'But you can rewire this handset so all our calls are free?'

'I could,' she says. 'But I won't unless it becomes a financial necessity.'

'Go on. Do it,' I encourage.

'I might.'

Dida's currently a victim of industry downsizing. A couple of agencies take her resumé and promise occasional short-term work. She follows the career path of our generation: undergraduate studies, graduate degrees, brief industry experience, under-employment.

I like Dida so much I avoid sleeping with everyone else. I like kissing so much that I eat more rarely than in the past. I never know what time it is. I close the door on Muffy, my dog, who scratches at it and whines for a few minutes.

Dida says, 'Aw, let him in,' but he jumps straight onto the bed and I make Dida lock him out, just to prove the point. After that we don't fuck for over an hour, such is the tension between us. And then, of course, we do, with even more passion and fury and relief. We sleep for twenty-five minutes, wake up, and I'm ready to hit the town. Come on, Dida. Let's go eat some more ice cream. Let's have a coffee with cream and sugar. Let's live it rich and sweet. We step into the lift. The lights above the lift door in the lobby count 7, 6, 5, 4, 3, 2, 1. (Important background information: what Australians call ground, New Yorkers call 1st floor.) The doors open. We step out into the lobby. We leave the apartment building and, although

9

my bedroom could be anywhere in the world, outside we are in New York.

Over butter-pecan ice cream and American coffee, Dida tells me she has me figured out and that I really am a bastard and that she likes me, maybe loves me, must remember never to trust me and to supervise what I wear should she happen to introduce me to her friends or family. I tell her I unequivocally love her but have no idea who she is or what she thinks. She tells me she has analysed my functions and that left to myself I would sleep precisely eight hours fifteen minutes per night and would often forget to breakfast. She explains that my attachment to Muffy is due to the dog's disrespect for property and that my own materialism is a projection of self-hatred. She tells me she likes me most when I forget to speak and least when I purposefully refrain from it.

She says, 'Try loving me now,' and she's right, I really can't love her at that moment.

Next she says, 'I like how your eyes flick from side to side when I manipulate you,' and I love her again.

We go to her place and pull all the alcohol out of the refrigerator: vodka, vodka, vodka. Really, Dida, no soda? Then we get really drunk and I call up Phil, my neighbour who keeps my spare key, and ask him to feed Muffy because I'm too drunk to go home and sorry it wasn't meant to happen it won't happen again. I hang up before he can complain or decide to say no. Dida lectures me on how to train Muffy to feed himself then go on to college.

Another good thing is never to look through the view-finder whilst pressing the shutter. Always shoot from the hip. In this way, late the next morning, I shoot a whole roll of pictures of Dida in the park. And she actually appears in almost all of them. When I show her the photographs she can't believe it (this is on a 2-train, uptown).

'You shot all these?' she says.

We discuss whether such pictures need to be flattering or whether the action of shooting a whole roll constitutes flattery enough.

'Anyway, in these ones, you look really nice,' I say.

'Yeah,' says Dida. 'I do.'

We kiss for a while and miss the subway stop, and miss it going back too, so we decide to skip the movie and have Chinese food in the East Village instead.

You know, I have never in my life seen anyone other than me or Dida kiss in the subway. What is wrong with the people in this city? What is their problem? It is too goddamn hot is what. We hide in a restaurant and eat chow mein with big spoons. Then we give all our change to a one-legged man and take the bus to Dida's apartment, collect a month's clothing and walk around to my apartment with suitcases in all our hands. Muffy is so pleased to see us he urinates on yesterday's *New York Times*, all over a front-page picture of ex-President George Bush.

I play my answering-machine tape. My ex-boss who thinks he is still my boss has left a message: 'Eisie here. Hope everything's OK. Do give me a call soon. EIC is looking forward to your return, too.'

'Eisenhower, the insincere bastard,' I say out loud.

'But sweetie,' soothes Dida, stroking my cheek, 'he died in nineteen sixty-nine.'

I explain that I don't mean Dwight D. Eisenhower but Eisenhower S~, the manager of the news section and a man with no personality. EIC is the Editor in Chief. We pronounce it 'eek', because for him everything is a crisis to be exclaimed over. EIC is a major reason for absenteeism. In this, he leads by example. Most of [Newspaper]'s employees and contractors have yet to meet him. He is an absent presence, an unseen force forever issuing edicts which are announced by various underlings who claim to have got the Word from him. He's a business type who must have thought newspapers would be a good next-step career move, and probably phrased it 'self-diversification'. No matter what his management representatives say at the new-style, all-hold-hands staff meetings, EIC means us to understand, 'Bottom line, think about the bottom line.'

The next day, Muffy and I walk in the park. I am thinking about Dida's body. I do not know what is in Muffy's mind. We see a panama hat skimming along the crest of a small rise. A head presses the hat into the air and two people are coming towards us. The man in the hat and bow tie is forty-five years old. He is walking with a bow-legged 28-year-old Spanish–American woman. The man in the panama hat is Steve M~, with whom I irregularly have telephone conversations. We met in this park a year before and spoke about the difficulty of being both blind and stylish. He said he hoped his blindness could be an element of his style, along with his bow tie.

'A bow tie,' he said, 'also has a tactile presence. It is something appropriate for a blind man to wear.'

At the end of that first conversation, I gave him the panama hat I had brought with me from Australia. He skimmed the hat's rim with his fingertips, thanked me, handed me his calling card, and placed the hat on his head at an intentionally or unintentionally jaunty angle.

'Hello,' I greet him this day. He introduces me to the woman, Julia (that's something like Hulia, for the non-Hispanics). I get the full story: the reason they are walking together is that Steve became disoriented after he tripped over a rock and hit his head on the path. The hat flew off and Steve was unable to retrieve it on his own. Julia, who recovered the hat for him, is assisting him to Fifth Avenue at 91st Street. Steve is going to his sister's birthday party on East 91st Street. Her name is Beatrice and she's forty-nine years old. These days, Steve characteristically wears the panama hat and keeps his bus pass in the hat band: Steve's head holds that tiny piece of Australia in the air above New York.

Julia had gone to the park to look for Phil, who fed Muffy a couple of days ago and lives next door to me. We discover this when Julia says she's about to meet someone and Steve says, 'She's meeting Phil. Vernon is Phil's neighbour,' and we say what a coincidence. The conversation finishes.

'Have a good time,' I tell Steve, and, to Julia, 'very nice to meet you.'

'Talk to you later,' Steve says.

Phil was supposed to meet Julia at the southeast entrance to the running track around the reservoir, but he won't make it because he has been called to Detroit on business and was unable to contact Julia to let her know although he tried four times, all day Monday, when Julia was at work, having forgotten to buy an answering machine on which he could leave a message. So, he is in Detroit feeling bad about Julia and at the same time blaming her.

I know all this because that night, just as Dida and I are getting into the bath, Julia rings the doorbell because Phil hasn't answered his door. She tells me her side of the story—I say, despite not knowing, 'That doesn't sound like Phil at all'. She also recounts her entire conversation with Steve in which she had tried to describe the relations between colours in terms of sound, taste and texture.

I tell her Phil had asked me to call her (not true) but that I had misplaced her number (not true) and that I was terribly sorry (such an apologetic guy I am) and, really, I must go to sleep now because I need to be up at 3 a.m., the best time to collect the eggs from the free range because it is when the chickens are most docile (would you believe). She leaves, looking sceptical. I climb into the bath with Dida and we close our eyes and talk about blindness.

Phil returns from Detroit the next day, asks me if I've seen Julia, fills me in on the story from his perspective. I tell him it sounds dubious, but wish him luck. He returns home and calls Julia. She hangs up on him. He calls her every fifteen minutes until she agrees to meet him. Much later, they have six children together, in Maryland of all places. But that's another story.

When I first moved to New York from Sydney, Australia, I stayed in a little hotel decorated with scars. This was near Gramercy Square, in 1983. Governments were still falling all over the world at the instigation of US agents, the Dutchman in the next room said. The hotel was tenanted with politically conscious foreigners. The lobby was hung with black and white photographs of scarred people: an old man stretching his loose skin tight to show the marks passing from behind his left shoulder, under his armpit and down his tattooed chest; a tired young man smiling, the scar taking his smile to his ear; a middle-aged woman showing the marks on the palm of her right hand and the back of her left hand, which divided each hand in two from between the median and ring fingers to the heel. There was a young woman with a welt on her biceps as thick as a thumb. Twins showed matching marks on their wrists.

My room was four floors up. I stayed there a month, until I found work selling silverware (what I used to call 'cutlery') in a department store. They hired me because the supervisor thought my accent charming and because I claimed to have four years' retail experience, mostly in silverware.

When I had furnished my apartment with silverware, I asked for a transfer to the china department. The other tenants in my building ate only from paper plates and I assumed china was prohibitively expensive for a young Australian taking up expatriatism. It probably would have been. Anyway, I did OK in this way, moving from department to department, but lost the job just prior to transferring to electricals. The firm was downsizing, nothing to do with the goods that walked, and I was never suspected.

I survived between jobs pawning silverware.

After that I was in service industries for a while, mostly bartending or waiting on restaurant tables.

In 1986 I got a lucky break, a job at a major metropolitan daily as a copy boy. As I've already mentioned, because of pending legal action there's not too much I can say about that particular publication. I will say, though, that I still really hate the letters columns. I really hate them. I hate that newspapers let people have opinions and I hate what those opinions are. What those opinions are is representative of the opinions of a whole lot of other people. Every word spoken tries to include me in it. I hate that. If I want to speak, I'll say what I want to say right in the middle of the op-ed page.

At [Newspaper], I worked my way up to the post of senior news editor. A senior news editor is someone who has developed a recognisable name and strong views, as a result of which he or she ceases to write news and, instead, 'expresses'. The day after my promotion, I too became opinionated. I earned a photo by-line. Management complimented me on the strength of my opinions. Internal memos arrived on my desk and through my e-mail: 'I admired the robustness of today's piece on the mayor', 'Terrific writing, Vernon' and 'I believe you speak for most Americans when you criticise the conditions of Manhattan's pavements'.

Career path is not my strength, and opinions bore me shitless, so I applied for and received a sideways move to senior sub-editor. I still wrote occasional opinion pieces, but mostly spent my time fucking up other people's work.

Crucially, following my shift of role, more people bought [Newspaper] each day. Not hundreds of thousands, but a measurable few per cent. Even more crucially, [Newspaper] management noticed.

'You're a marvel, Vern,' I was told more than once, 'a fucking freak with the journalistic vocabulary.'

I sure was. I added that vital Australian touch, that mildest shift of accent. Through me, [Newspaper] acquired accessible, non-threatening allure.

And then I met Dida in the park and stopped attending. My only excursions now are walkies with doggo.

Muffy is extremely excitable recently. Occasionally on our walks, he starts to barking and keeps on barking until every dog in whatever neighbourhood we've walked to is yapping away.

Muffy: *A skinny old guy crosses Lexington at 23rd, with the lights, and he's screaming in a cracked high voice the whole time and I can hear him from way up the other side of 24th and he's screaming, 'Oh sure, drunk again in the middle of the street, crazy old man, why don't you get back on to the sidewalk until the signals go green, what are you, crazy?' And he's screaming so loud that I don't know how he can sustain it but he goes on, 'You're drunk, aren't you, you dumb drunk bastard, and you're out in the middle of the traffic and you'll be run down, yes you will you crazy old man, you're gonna be knocked over,' and then he reaches the sidewalk and stops.*

Since my resignation from [Newspaper] did not occur in the prescribed manner, [Newspaper]'s accounts department is not terribly interested in helping me out with severance pay.

'We haven't received a request on the approved form,' a pay officer explains. 'We're not in the business of giving money away, you know.'

Fuck 'em, if that's their attitude.

'I don't need to talk to them any more,' I tell Dida. 'And I don't want to, either.'

Dida insists I chase it up.

'They owe it to you, after all these years. Let them put out an extra advertising supplement. And Vernon: you think I'd do this with an undischarged bankrupt?' is the clincher, as she tucks her hand down the front of my shorts.

I call Eisie.

'Vern! It's so good to hear from you, cobber,' he drawls, fake-sincerely.

'Yeah, you too,' I say, though I can hardly remember him already. 'How's it going over there? Listen, Eisie, I need my severance pay. Can you organise it, send me the forms or whatever?'

'I'd really like to help you out,' he lies in return, 'but I'm instructed you're in breach of contract, so I must ask you to return to work.'

'I can't do that.' I fail to explain that I actually could return but won't, or that the forces preventing my return are either (a) internal and self-directed or (b) (i) due to Dida's irresistible charms and (ii) no, you don't know her.

'Let me know when you change your mind.' He hangs up.

Ah well, I think, no doubt had I attempted to resign properly, my explanation wouldn't have corresponded with any of the available 'Reasons for Termination' boxes on the relevant form.

Next step: I repeatedly dial an attorney's listed Manhattan number and still cannot succeed to understand the short recorded message before the telephone goes dead. Something to add to my list of experiences of foreignness. After five or six attempts, I go ask Dida to listen for me. She says the recording says 'error in number'. I try another firm, but they refuse to represent me, citing 'possible conflicts of interest' and meaning, 'One day, we hope to represent your antagonists.' Eventually, Mann McKenzie Michaels offers to take me as a client provided I forward a deposit within seven (7) days.

'No can do,' I tell the receptionist. 'How about payment upon success?'

'Well, sir, I'm afraid we cannot be of assistance,' I am told.

I give up on the idea. I no longer have a taxable income, so good ol' slogans like 'no taxation without representation' don't help either. The lesson I should have but probably haven't learned from this is that a professional should only leave a job if he or she has another one lined up one hundred per cent. Law firms will not credit, 'But I've never felt like this with anyone else,' as they do cold, comfortable cash. I tell Dida how the lawyers won't be my friends and beg her not to leave me. She says, 'Well, OK. But if you're declared bankrupt a second time within the next twenty-five years, I will not be so lenient.'

'That'll never happen,' I say, gesturing towards my work desk with an elbow. 'We'll live off the proceeds of [Newspaper]'s word-processing equipment. I know just the pawnbroker.'

Everything of value on my desk, plus the desk itself, once belonged to [Newspaper]. I used to consider these items perks of the job. Now, I decide, I will think of them as superannuation.

I'm learning all the time what it is to be American. Excuse me, sir. Can you tell me how to get to Broadway? Practise, my friend.

With Dida, I feel invincible and invisible. We are all there is, I think. At a ritual flag ceremony for some American national day, I buy and wear a badge that looks like this:

and that really upsets everybody, especially because I am foreign and have no right to judge so harshly. Dida laughs and laughs at the faces people pull: turning bright red, lips twitching. Finally, a red-faced, obscenity-muttering, barrel-chested man in a mid-grey suit tears the badge off me and a big hole in my shirt, too.

I say, 'So much for the First Amendment.'

Thinking I am British because of my Australian accent, the ignorant pig demands, 'Didn't you fuckers learn anything from the Boston Tea Party?'

I say (in my plummiest tone), 'Yes. Of course. We learned that we should have taught you some manners before allowing you to retain this colony.'

He takes a swing at me then, so Dida drags me away through the crowd, badgeless and holey shirted, and at the other side she starts shouting stuff at me like, 'Well that was pretty goddamn stupid, wasn't it?'

I am a bit stunned so I start laughing like crazy instead of speaking and I laugh until I have recovered enough to grab Dida's hand, pull her into a diner and order blueberry muffins. She kind of slumps into her chair, shaking her head.

She says, 'You're a crazy fucker, you're fucking crazy.'

I start swearing at her too and we are sitting in this little diner with mouths full of blueberry muffin spraying expletives at each other and of course we start laughing again and choking and tears are streaming down our cheeks because we can't get any air down our windpipes. Then all the waiters come out and start slapping us on the backs so we swear at them too and the tall one calls me a dumbfuck Aussie and I say, 'Could you tell from my accent?' and he says, 'No, from the fucking stupid way you choke on your muffin.' Then we all go out back to the kitchen and drink ourselves completely loopy on Mexican and Canadian beer and hours later the short waiter drives us very shakily home and we make it just inside the door before we tear each other's clothes off and fall into each other in the hallway. Actually, I don't remember that bit at all, only waking up sometime later with a chill down my left side. I shake Dida and we stumble into bed again.

Most times Dida goes out, the telephone rings. Although she purports to be doing freelance phone repairs, this is merely an excuse for trying out other voices on me.

'It always sounds like you,' I say.

'I do not,' she says.

Then she goes out. I don't see her for the rest of the day, but she telephones every half hour or so with another accent, or a deeper sound, or a throatier one.

'Definitely, definitely unrecognisable,' I say at one stage. She later denies that that particular voice (Eastern European) had been her.

'Who else could it have been?' I ask.

Dida shrugs. 'How would I know?'

Usually when I leave the apartment, it is in the company of Muffy. Occasionally I go on my own. Sometimes Dida and I go places together, and sometimes the three of us go play in the park. Post-employment life is definitely superior to vocational pursuits. I try catching up by phone with a few friends. I make Phil the neighbour have conversations with me. I harass former colleagues. Most days I sit down to proofread [Newspaper]. I circle typographical mistakes and poor phrasing and post the corrected version anonymously to Eisie.

When I return home after one trip to the post office, there's a record on. Muffy's barking like crazy because he cannot stand the sound of slide guitar. People downstairs are screaming at each other.

'Hey!' Dida interrupts the cacophony. 'Let's go hear

some music. There's a famous saxophonist supported by a famous recording company's recording artist in a famous jazz club in the Village.'

So we go down to the Village and do that.

We sit at a table. The music begins.

'The saxophonist has the hottest acoustic bassist I've ever seen,' I shriek.

'Isn't that [indecipherable]?' says someone at the next table who's with someone with a V.I.P. card.

'Hey it is. I didn't recognise him without the moustache. He's shaved off his moustache.'

The waitress comes over and says to the V.I.P., 'Are you Big Uncle?'

'That's right!' he says, grinning. I focus on his V.I.P. card and it really does say 'Big Uncle' on it.

'Nice to see you,' she says, and goes away again.

Then the Famous Recording Company's recording artist starts playing. His group wears suits and he introduces each song in a loud clear voice, as in, 'That was SAWNG by the great SAWNGWRITER.' The other two people at our table spend the evening staring at each other and saying things like, 'I was just thinking how lucky I am to have met you.'

Dida and I sit opposite each other with our legs tangled up. I stare at the bass player and she stares at the drummer. They're both perspiring like crazy. The music is really jumping. We considerably exceed the two-drink minimum by the end of the set, but maintain some decorum, and do not harass the young couple by speaking to them about anything.

After the set, we go home and switch on the TV in the bedroom. The anchor says, 'Another cab driver shot in Brooklyn. But this one lived to tell the tale, live and exclusive.' They cross to the hospital bed.

'Tonight has been a total New York experience,'

I tell Dida. 'Thank you for sharing it with a half-foreigner like me.'

'Aw shucks,' she says. 'I woulda shared it with you even if you'd been from New Jersey.'

Muffy (locked out of the bedroom, listening to the radio): *They've developed all these new types of barbed wire. You'd really cut yourself up trying to cross that, really hurt yourself bad. How long, if all the people were removed, would it take plants to wipe out all the evidence of city, moss and grasses to break up the streets, shrubs to collapse the skyscrapers? How long would it take the ivy to cover over the barbed wire, to replace all this orderly fencing with wild and spontaneous hedges, for nature's security system to supercede humans' redundant attempts at self-protection?*

We wake up on a Tuesday and roll into each other's arms, legs, bodies. I'm surprised as always to find Dida beside me. Every night I forget about her just before I wake up. I tell her that. She tells me how much my ass perspires. I try to pattern her body with goose bumps through selective nipping. She seizes my nose with her teeth and holds it just tight enough so I cannot move. Then she starts tickling me. I'm lying there shouting, 'Pax! Pax!' but it sounds too ridiculous with a blocked nose.

Later on, we borrow Phil's car.

'Well I guess you can use it,' Phil says. 'It's not the sort of favour I'd ask anyone for.'

'Thanks a lot,' I tell him, holding out my hand for the keys. 'If ever you need anything from me, you're welcome to it.'

We get out of the city for the day, to this really neat wooded area on Long Island a couple of hours north. Dida and her friends go there all the time.

An unwelcoming sign greets us: NO DOGS.

'Whoops, I'd forgotten all about that,' says Dida.

'Hello there,' says a ranger. 'You'd like me to look after your dog, I suppose. I wish you people wouldn't bring animals up here. I really do.'

'Sorry,' we mumble.

We leave Muffy in a little wire enclosure beside the ranger's hut. The poor little dog is enraged at driving all that way to sit behind a fence when there are so many squirrels outside, but really Muffy, we didn't know. None of Dida's friends had ever tried to bring a little white dog here before. If we had known the ranger's attitude, we would've gone somewhere you could have run around too. Muffy will not be comforted. His ears droop and he looks up at us with deep sadness and, possibly, resentment.

'Sorry, Muffy,' I whisper. 'We'll be back real soon. Bye-bye.' Dida flutters her fingers at him.

Dida and I set off down a wide trail totally covered with leaves and twigs. A half-hour into our walk, Dida sees something to one side of the trail.

'Look,' she says. 'Will you look at that. It might be a little white animal, but it is refraining from movement.'

'It might be nothing at all,' I tell her. I am trying to follow her gesture down a slope.

'I'm going down there to see for myself,' she says.

I finally see where and what it is.

'Honey,' I say, protectively (I'd never called her that before). 'Dida, that is a panama hat.'

'You are right,' she says. 'I thought it looked strangely familiar.' She pauses, then says, 'I'm going down there anyway.' When she reaches the hat, she picks it up and turns it over. 'It says, "Made in Australia",' she calls. She returns to the trail and holds the hat towards me. I take it and turn it over. There is a small, rust-like stain inside, where the hat would touch the temple.

'I think this could be blood,' I say, wrinkling my nose.

CHAPTER 2

We take the panama hat home with us and I put it on the TV. I try to call Steve to let him know we've found it. It's probably his hat. I try to telephone him a couple more times. The guy's never home, and I begin to tire of his inane answering-machine message: 'Leave your name and number and I'll get back to you. See you later. Ha-ha!'

Anyway, perhaps the mark is something other than blood. Could be the bloodstain's not so much a blood-stain as a sign of Steve's profuse perspiring, or a problem with the dye. When we watch TV, the hat becomes a comic distraction from every close-up shot. Ninety-five per cent of interview subjects appear ridiculous when they float four inches below a panama. After a few days, I move the hat to the top of the bookshelf beside the TV, out of the way. It stays there for a couple of weeks, but late at night I see it in my peripheral vision and start, 'Who's that?' Every time I'm a little fatigued, I get the sense of someone else in the room besides Dida or Muffy. Over time, this feeling becomes more disturbing than the extremely slight possibility that the discolouration inside the hat-rim is an indication of some action beyond sweating. I take the hat from the bookshelf and put it on top of the wardrobe in the bedroom, where it's not so much of an eye-catcher.

I won't say that I forget about the blind man's hat, but Dida is pretty distracting. I lose touch with the mundanities of work, regular hours, proper meals, and maintenance of secondary friendships and acquaintanceships. I do not mind.

After a few more totally distracted weeks, there is a paper snowdrift of mail across the apartment's front hall. It's snow in that we keep skidding across it, losing our footing. Eventually I throw most of it out unread, though I keep an eye out for [Newspaper]'s stationery. I had hoped [Newspaper] would relent on the severance pay. Also, if I was lucky, a salary cheque processed by the slow-learning automated pay system might turn up. Neither arrives. Instead, the first letter with the company trademark on the envelope is this:

Contractual Enforcement Services
Licensed Corporate Agents
21 Second Avenue, Unit 113

August 2, 199~

Our Ref: 9994 6501 R31782 EST 06/05/9~
Your Ref: MR VERNON COLLINS

PLEASE READ THIS—IMPORTANT
$69 248 DAMAGES AND EXPENSES FOR BREACH
OF CONTRACT
REFERENCE FILE 9994 6501 R31782
ESTABLISHED 06/05/9~

\# You owe money to [Newspaper] for failure to fulfil obligations under contract for service.
\# [Newspaper] has instructed us to obtain the sum of $69 248.

YOU HAVE 3 CHOICES: Send us THE MONEY IN FULL.
OR: CONTACT US IMMEDIATELY and make REASONABLE ARRANGEMENTS TO PAY the account.
OR: FULFIL YOUR OBLIGATIONS under your current contract.

Should you not respond within 7 DAYS we can ISSUE A SUMMONS and have THE MONEY taken out of your PROPERTY.

We don't want to sue you so PLEASE SEND YOUR MONEY NOW.

FOR YOUR CONVENIENCE, YOUR CREDIT CARD CAN BE USED TO SETTLE THE ACCOUNT IF REQUIRED.

Yours faithfully,
Collection Agent,
Collection Division—Contractual Enforcement Services

I rip it in two and drop it on the floor.

'I guess that wasn't a thank-you note,' Dida comments.

I show her it and add, 'I'm not even going to think of replying to the lousy, blackmailing son of a bitch.'

Dida tarantaras, 'C'mon, burn the flag,' like it's our new go-get-'em war cry. 'Remember, Vern, *you* wore that badge. What an act of defiance that was. I thought you were all for the First Amendment.'

'Yeah. Right,' I grumble.

I no longer enjoy the United States mail service. I can remember a time, soon after I switched countries, when the mail carried connections with people back home. Most correspondences these days are within the USA. I used to think of letters as hands linked across the water. Nowadays, letters are hooks at the ends of unbreakable lines, and all connections are involuntary.

Until today, though, I had not been subjected to letters of demand and unsolicited threats. The worst aspect is that my former colleagues must have initiated this action. I did lunch with these people, laughed at culture jokes at my expense and tried to convince them that the world has many centres while they replied, 'Bullshit, Vernon. How can you live on Manhattan and think that?'

Now I can only write defensive letters. I'm even reluctant to do that, but Dida convinces me and I let her.

I acknowledge, 'Your role is to talk me into things.'

'And to make sure you capitulate to no one else.'

I write the reply and wait until the seven days mentioned in the collection agency's letter are up. I post it.

Parkinson Pewley and Pierce
Attorneys at Law
Suites 21–26 Princely Tower
86 Fifth Avenue
New York City

Without prejudice

10th August 199~

Mr Eisenhower T. S~
[Newspaper]
NYC

Dear Eisie,

Your debt collectors sent our client Mr Vernon
Collins this letter (pieces enclosed). You've got to
be joking. While at one time in the past our
client was paid by you and even signed a contract of employment, he is now neither
interested nor liable.

He has no intention of paying any amount, let
alone returning to work with your organisation.
Please call your debt collectors off.

As you know, or ought to know, you owe money
to him. With regard to this sum, expect to hear
further from us in the near future.

Yours sincerely,

Harry X. Pewley

'Pewley?' queries Dida.
   'It's a very good name for a lawyer.'
   'It's a little too meta.'
   'You think newspaper people have any sense of
irony? I've worked with them and I can tell you they
don't. And the letterhead looks fantastic.'
   'Parkinson or Pierce would be better.'
   'I'm sticking with Pewley. I like it,' I say, defensively.
   'Well, what's the X stand for?'
   'I haven't thought it through that far.'
   'You are the most corrupt lover I've ever had.'

'You have obviously known no other journalists.'

My tactic is neither effective nor ineffective. My former boss probably snubs my fictitious representatives at their fictitious address, but he sets some powerless subordinate the task of ignoring me. A reply arrives at my address very shortly after, which at least indicates that my ex-colleagues feel some urgency, that they believe ignoring is an active task.

WITHOUT PREJUDICE

August 12, 199~

Re: [Newspaper] Ref: 31782
Dear Mr Collins

Thank you for your letter of August 10. While I sympathise with the position you and others like you claim to be in, the onus is on you to establish any discharge or waiver of contract you wish [Newspaper] to take into consideration in its dealings with you.

See you back at the office. Otherwise, as mentioned in our collection agency's letter, we'll be seeing you in court. Note that continuation of any close [Newspaper]-based working relationships and/or friendships is contingent on your acceptance of the conditions set out in that letter. (Further note that this organisation is on to you concerning missing office equipment. The Property Department will pursue this matter on its own account.)

Your faithful servant,
Joe Tresidio

enc: all previous correspondence on this matter

When corporate bullies decide to pick on you, the only contribution you can make is to worry. This helps them enormously. Dida and I decide against assisting [Newspaper] in this regard. We discuss next moves, and decide that if [Newspaper] intends vigorously to refrain from acknowledging my protests and claims, I will neglect to undertake any further response to them. Let the corporate bastards do all the work. I've made my point. I could try to get a real lawyer again, but it's not yet necessary. Harry Pewley, were he to exist, would know what to do.

Meantime, Dida and I have other diversions: each other. We see no one else for a week.

'Submit, submit,' Dida calls from the bedroom. My penis leads me to her, as though she's tied a cord around it.

'It's a hundred miles of silk,' she notes as we entangle. 'It's the world's stickiest gossamer, and I'm going to bite through your nervous system.'

In the middle of the confusion of webbing and limbs which follows, the phone rings. Typical. The way to attract telephone calls is frequent fucking. We pay no attention to it, of course. The answering machine etc.

Some unmeasured time later, I play the message. It sounds like it's spoken through a couple of layers of ceiling insulation: 'Page B6, column three, first word lines seven through eleven.'

Terrific. Now we'll have to buy today's [Newspaper] and bring to an end our perpetual and blissful nakedness.

'Come on, Dida, let's all go.'

In a barrage of 'no way's and 'it's your friend's, Dida refuses to dress. I find some jeans and a shirt.

'Well, Muffy, it's you and me, little dog. Let's take a whizz in the street for once.'

Muffy is just too happy. The lift nearly gets Muffy's newspaper treatment, too. No, Muffy, no. No. Good boy.

Muffy: *I'm so confounded. Everyone says yes to me. Or sometimes no. I am not certain which is the more prevalent. In my mind I circle and circle. Nothing sets to decision. The streets seem to lead to the horizon and yet I always return to my point of departure. The people maintain similarities but I only know one person, and his patterns are erratic.*

The message in [Newspaper] reads, 'pay. for Our mistakes ver'—with 'ver' the second half of an awkward hyphenation of 'Oliver'. Not many people know me as 'Ver', but it must refer to me. Someone powerful enough to bypass sub-editing is very angry.

Worse still, beside an adjacent story headed 'Blind Man Missing' is a photograph of Steve. No one has seen him since the day I encountered him on his way to his sister's. As my brain tells itself, 'Oh shit,' I realise two things. Steve's absence is very serious: something bad has happened to him. Also, through juxtaposing the two pieces, [Newspaper] is physically threatening me.

Back in the apartment, Dida and I re-read and re-read the two pieces, one the orthodox article, and one, of only five words, newly realised in highlighter felt-pen.

'Poor Steve,' says Dida.

'Yes. Poor Steve,' I say. 'Poor Steve, too.'

We guess that our self-imposed retreat has provoked the linking of the threat, if that's what it is, with the news of Steve's disappearance. There is no immediately available or feasible alternative. Why else would the two articles appear so close together? There is the coincidence of person: I both know Steve and am 'ver'. And the near coincidence of time: Steve was last seen by friends not long after I was last seen at [Newspaper].

Some things are too frightening to contemplate for long. Dida and I can see no way through. Instead of engaging directly with the articles, we try to get out more often, and so avoid the issue altogether. We see other people or, at least, restaurants. The telephone has been ringing late at night. We answer, but no one is ever there: only an emptiness which after endless repetitions becomes more and more threatening. As a tactical response, we check out every eating place south of Houston, leaving no one home but the machine, which we have taught to say: 'Hello, leave a (bark, bark) message which I might give to the people but I might not because I'm technologically redundant.'

On my own, I take to answering the telephone: 'Harassed and Confused Employment Agency. Good afternoon.'

One time it is Phil, the neighbour, on the other end: had we borrowed his welcome mat for some reason? No, we hadn't. If we find it, can we give it back? No problem.

'Muffy . . . ? What have you been up to?'

Muffy looks far too innocent to trust with this one.

When Dida overhears my new telephone-answering technique, she gives me a blast: 'What are you doing talking to these hoodlums like that, you class-A demi-moron? These people are professionals.'

And I say, 'Yeah, well, you can probably tell that from the tone of their silences. If they don't want me to treat them with jocularity, they better say who they are and why they deserve respect. Anyway, that was Phil.'

I'm seriously pissed, and she has to agree with me on that one: 'these people' are no more articulate than any other anonymous, heavy-breathing pho-nophilomaniacs.

Threatening phone calls and the two newspaper items concentrate our minds on my contractual break-down, but also again on Steve's hat, if that's whose it is, as seems increasingly likely. It comes to stand in for the blind man's disappearance, for [Newspaper]'s harassment of me, and for any possible connection between the two. The hat is becoming ever more of an iconic presence, there, on top of the wardrobe in our bedroom.

I had half-suggested taking it to the police, but as Dida argued, 'They'll just lose it. It's too refutable as evidence at the moment. Besides, according to the police shows, eleven per cent of New York City police officers are on the make. Too great a risk until we've got more and stronger material to present.'

We decide to keep it, at least for the moment. With [Newspaper] already threatening legal action against me, I am all for being convinced of the need for police-avoidance. Also, there is something hero-sexy about the missing man's hat on the wardrobe in the bedroom.

So, on with the new routine. Come on, Muffy, wel-come to the exercise-rich lifestyle of the employment-deprived. Let's go walk past all those rejected employers panting at their windows after Dida and me and, damn it all, you, you supersmart little hyperdawg.

Muffy: *Gridlock, grid unlock. Chance manoeuvres in the Ur-metropolis. Blah blah blah. I don't buy it. Isn't*

Manhattan just the cutest microchip, all these avenues from One up and streets the same? All cabs the one colour and people in gradations from albino to ebony and their clothing full of references to the visible spectrum and sounds vibrating all over the place like boooom boooom and tweetweetwee and ssssss. This sweet little insect island with the bridges like tiny, entomorphic legs and antennae and tentacles and irradiated capillaries. Aah, New York, the rich tapestry of human existence strung together with any old cotton.

After the walk, Dida comes up with the ideal post-employment project.

'I'm going to find that blind guy,' decides Dida. 'He's probably sitting hatlessly in the shade, so that cuts out half the places to look. Even if he's dead, he's probably lying in the shade. I think I'm already on the trail. You with me?'

'I'm with you,' I tell her, 'but let's take a break for an hour or so.'

'Forty-five minutes,' she says, and I can tell she means it.

I remember Steve's sister's name from seeing Steve in the park, which was just before he disappeared. We find her address in the Manhattan telephone directory. We walk across town and through the park to Beatrice's apartment. Sorry, Muffy, you'll have to wait at the gate. Muffy whines as I tie him up. We ring the doorbell. A woman whom we know to be forty-nine years old opens the door the full four inches of the security chain.

'Uh, hi. Er, sorry to disturb you, but, er, Beatrice, we're ah, we're, um, friends of your brother. Your brother's.'

'Stevie. Mm-hmm. So?' She's peering at us through the narrow gap.

'Mm. And we want to help, er, locate him. You know. Um. We hear he hasn't been seen for a while.'

'Mmm.'

'Yes. Can we, like, talk to you about him—Steve—Stevie—for a few minutes?'

'I'll be with you momentarily.'

The door closes. A few minutes pass. The door unlatches and opens. 'Won't you come in?'

'Thank you very much, Beatrice,' says Dida.

'Bea. Please.'

'Thank you,' I say. 'Stay, Muffy. Staaaa-aay. Siiiiiiit.'

The living area is very nice. There is some furniture and a window. It says a lot about Bea and, more importantly, about Steve's family. Bea is wearing nice clothes, comfortable, useful.

I sit down on a nice chair and think, What the hell am I doing here? I don't know what to ask this person. I'm a total fraud who is more likely to make very much worse whatever anxiety this nice woman is feeling. I sit on the nice chair trying to sort out how to leave without appearing too insane, and I hardly notice Dida switch into the good-cop routine. I must be the silent, awkward one. I'm a natural for the part. Really.

'Of course,' says Dida, 'many people "disappear" for a few days simply because they want to take a break from their routines. It's generally nothing to worry about, Bea. But Bea, it would be good to know, has he done this sort of thing before?'

Dida's practically calling her 'ma'am'. You can pretty much hear the pauses where she could have called her that. Bea responds as if Dida's behaviour is perfectly natural, but I'm cowering into my chair, attempting chameleonisation.

'Not that I know of. Certainly, if he's said he's coming to my birthday he always has in the past.'

'Has he been under any pressure recently? Anything he mentioned to you, Bea?'

She asks it with sensitivity capitalised all over her tone. I cannot believe Dida is doing this. I'm now trying to look focused rather than absent; silent, rather than stoopid. Dida has a notepad. She's playin' the whole 'we're "friends" who might be able to help' charade. Under her plain clothes she must have on her superhero bustier, with CopWoman embroidered in gold tinsel.

'Well, he didn't mention anything.'

'He would tell you . . . ? Please, Bea, I know these questions are difficult.'

'There's no reason he wouldn't.'

I excuse myself: I have to check on the dog. If I had been Dida, I probably would have cased the freestanding 'robe in the entrance hall on my way outside.

Dida emerges half an hour later. Muffy and I have had a nice time playing snap-at-the-leaf. Muffy whinges because the game stops. Dida is very angry with me. I am holier than she. We both say 'that poor woman' to each other a few times. Dida won't admit that the visit was worse than useless—worse in that we have probably disturbed poor Beatrice further, given her additional worries—and I won't admit that we could, repeat, *could*, have gained valuable information leading to the rediscovery of Steve. What's more, I regret agreeing so readily to Dida's detective idea. It was fine in theory only.

When we get home, there is a message on the answering machine.

'Oh-ho. A message!' I sneer. 'A leeetle message. Well,

machine, this is your last chance to be friendly, or I'm going to tear your cord out and toss you in the trash.'

'Beeeeeeeeep. Please come back to thuh office. Please come back. Please. Beeep. Beeep. Beeep.'

I don't recognise the voice. Serious? Or a joke?

'Was that you?' I ask Dida, who snorts and goes into the kitchen. Was that you, Muffy, you clever, fluffy rat?

This message is an improvement on legal threats and late-night silences, anyway. I'm almost tempted to return. In a brief moment of economic rationality, I realise that the rent will one day come due and the bank account will no longer co-operate. Another month away, though. Aaah, fuck it. It can wait.

After Dida's Bea interrogation, I call her 'Sarge', as in, 'More coffee, Sarge?'

She says, 'Quit that. It's getting on my nerves,' and I say, 'Sure, Sarge,' and so on for another few days. When she realises I'm not going to quit, she starts in on calling me names too, a whole logical progression:

Jules (as in Verne/Vernon);

20K (as in *Twenty Thousand Leagues Under the Sea*), which is too long to sustain and which becomes, drunkenly:

Twinky, a terrific endearment and one which I never answer to;

Subbo, from submarine, from the Verne genealogy;

Sub, which, I moan, is the job I've escaped from, an argument to which she is surprisingly quite receptive;

Mariner, or Marro (ugh);

and Albatross ('The Rime of the Ancient _____'); with its twin diminutives Alby or Tross, an unspoken theory of verbal poetics no doubt underlying their alternation.

'What happened to proper, loving progressions, like

honey, hunky, hunky-wunky, wunky-woo-woo?' I complain.

'Is that how things go in Australia?' she retorts. She offers to turn me into a one-liner, as in, 'I've just taken up golf and this is my handicap.'

'Wow, that is soooo American,' I mock.

'You want I should call you "y'old bastard"? Would you prefer that?'

'Do you think we're bickering a lot these days, darling?' I sweeten.

'Aw, poor wounded Alby,' she puckers. 'Do the closets count as rooms? There are two or three built-ins we haven't done the horizontal slam-dance in yet.'

Every place in the apartment produces slightly different genital sensations. Despite the lack of fresh air, which an evolutionist might predict would cause desperate mortal conflict, we get on better and better. We resist the impulse to turn our experience into a philosophy of conflict resolution or to offer courses such as 'Love Your Way to a Happy Relationship'.

Instead, Dida is occupied trying to figure out who else to question about Steve. Bea has given her a list of his friends and their telephone numbers. Dida is working through them. Her opening gambit is: 'I'm not a crank, but . . .'

'The mystery to me is why you are so involved in this,' I tell her. 'Can you solve that one for me?'

She asks if I think she should stop and I say I didn't mean it like that, but it—I don't know—detection seems to be turning into a career and I'm wondering if that's what she wants at this point. After all, we could regard each other as fully occupying.

'You are unbelievable,' she tells me, shaking her head.

'You are incredible,' I say, trying to put the moon in my voice.

'Coy!' says Dida, but she becomes convinced of the room's nocturnal glow.

If [Newspaper]'s last attempt to woo me back is genuine, it is because they are hurting in the only place corporations can hurt. A rival newspaper has published a survey showing circulation of [Newspaper] falling and that of its rivals on the up and up. Survey question: 'Have you switched newspaper loyalties in the last month?' Seven per cent said yes, and ninety-two per cent of that shift was away from [Newspaper]. The rival newspaper's majority shareholder is quoted as saying, 'If we had experienced that sharp a decline, I'd be doing two things. First, I'd be asking a lot of goddamn questions. Two, I'd be looking very closely at advertising revenue.

'I think their current rates are unsustainable, especially when you see how much better our rates are, both on a per-ad basis and on audience reach for your advertising dollar.'

[Newspaper] ran a page A1 story noting that profits in the previous financial year were up twelve per cent on the back of circulation and consequent advertising revenue rises. The story failed to mention the rumour of a more recent fall in circulation. Nonetheless, stocks were down 14¢ to $4.66.

The next day, a second rival headed off with: 'Why New York Won't Buy [Newspaper]'. At the top of its survey list was 'unreliable', with a twenty-four per cent citing by loyalty-switchers. A related box was headed '[Newspaper] is "Dan Quayle" of Newspapers', with one respondent reportedly saying, 'My kids are learning reading and writing at school. I want them to see correctly spelled words in their daily papers. I want them to know how to spell "potato".' (Quayle, a former US Vice-President, had once flunked a spelling bee.) The first rival ran a page three story, '[Newspaper]: Rumours of Spellcheck Virus Denied'.

Neither rival picked up on the true extent of what [Newspaper] had lost through my absence. If only they realised that Australianness sold papers, they'd be trying their darnedest to get hold of some. It's an elusive quality: plenty of people have it, but I'm the only one who has managed to process it for newspaper readers.

Australia was this place where I grew from eight and a quarter pounds to one hundred fifty-eight, from a foot and a bit long to five feet ten, from a little sucker motivated by raw reflex and hunger to a big chewer driven by cooked experience. In that process I ingested immeasurable quantities of Australianness, that elusive yet demonstrably marketable characteristic. I brought [Newspaper] the Australian sense of physical emptiness and namelessness. The US of A fills its emptiness with national myths, and names all its heroes. Australia is built on the pretence of emptiness, that no one lived there when the British arrived: *terra nullius*. My self-suiting theory is that this pretence is reflected in the Australian intonation, syntax and choice of words. My rephrasings and rewritings combined with Americans' ever-ready sense of heroic nationalism to give [Newspaper] readers the flattering sense that they were explorers and conquerors, forever victorious. Unlike Australians, Americans pretend that the British didn't arrive, that the first European settlers unBritished themselves on the transatlantic journey and that it was *Americans* who landed in the New

World. Thus, the British later tried and failed to invade an already established nation.

My subbing gave [Newspaper] a modesty, an understatedness, a mild sense of retiring inferiority. Readers, unconsciously comparing themselves with the moderately Australian-accented voice of [Newspaper], felt great. This is what I'd remind my employers, anyhow.

In Australia, my problem had been that it felt wrong to take things. Everything had already been taken, and all that remained was to give it back. For me, Australia had no further material depth, no sense of glut, of available immoral surfeit. Maybe its atmosphere has changed in the last decade or so. Maybe not. To arrive in New York was a liberation. In NYC, I even stole myself a career.

'Look at this.' I wave the falling-circulation clippings at Dida. 'This is your fault.'

'So, my seduction of you is working,' she laughs. 'Come on, Muffy. Let's take a walk.'

Immediately, Muffy is scratching at the door like a maniac, saying, 'Yelp! Yelp! Yelp! Yelp! Yelp! Yelp! Yelp! Yelp! Yelp! Yelp! Yelp! Yelp!' while I'm trying to pull on my running shoes and Dida is shouting, 'OK! OK! We're going already!'

Muffy: *What's so tasteful about vents? All this steam returning to its rightful place, up: gases to gases and dust to dust. The city would be better off without them. You can never tell where a vent is going to turn up. Here you are walking along Park Avenue, and suddenly: a vent. There is a slight rise in temperature, but I'd prefer to run into a shop. The condensation happens up there in the sky somewhere, because there's no windscreen over this city, no restriction on the migratory movements of water molecules. I quite like left-over hotdogs. I also like certain sandwiches, provided there's no fish on them. I also like awnings. I like grass of between three and six inches in height. Barking is good.*

On our late-summer walks, Central Park remains exactly the same in its steady changingness. The trees grow, the grass grows, similar people wander or stride or jog or bicycle along the well-trodden paths and tracks. Dida and I kiss along the smooth, straight parts and feed little bits of ice cream to Muffy, who is trying to run in several directions at once and consequently spins and spins. He will not stop barking today. I give him an extra cone and he runs in circles barking with the cone unchewed in his mouth.

'Be careful. You'll choke on that,' I warn him, but he doesn't care. He finally swallows the cone and decides to urinate on every tree in the park, but not in order. Today, Muffy is a little, fluffy, rubber asteroid.

Dida becomes high-energy and says, 'You'll never catch up to me,' and runs off towards the Conservatory Garden, so I chase her and Muffy keeps running in front of my legs so I'm stopping and starting and Dida's turning around and running backwards and shouting, 'Run, Muffy, run,' like in some first-grade reading primer, and laughing, and Muffy's barking again and has stopped trying to be a one-dog nitrate factory, and I'm trying to step over him or run around him but he keeps moving much too fast and finally Dida, who's turning around to see if I'm catching up, trips over her leg and collapses and I fall onto the ground next to her, pretending that I'm not wheezing, just a little short of breath, and Muffy races off into some shrubbery and tosses half-rotted leaves between his hind legs for a few seconds. I feel perspiration osmosing to the surface of my skin, and mop at my forehead. Dida rests her head on my chest.

'Your heart's amazing. How can something that size move so quickly?' she gasps. 'Man, we should either exercise more, or else never at all.'

Muffy trots back with something unpleasant-looking in his mouth. It's muddy and slightly damp with dog spittle, but it's clearly Steve's bow tie.

'It's the bow tie,' we tell each other.

'Shit.'

Even after this many years, no one thinks I am a local. My accent is moving east, but it's still mid-Pacific, south of the big island of Hawaii, somewhere near the radioactive Mururoa Atoll. Americans call me 'mate' and make jokes about koalas. Australia is a couple of brandnames and an overfriendly attitude. I try to pour well-known US trademarks into my conversations. I never go to the store—I go to particular, as-advertised-on-TV, well-known marts. My jeans have US marks and so do my shirts and shoes. I try to like basketball and, not having managed to like it, try to pretend to like it. I am practically the same as any New Yorker you could meet. Yet people only ever notice my differences.

'You don't sound American,' I am told almost every day. 'Where y'all from?'

'I sound more American than anything else,' I tell them. 'I'm not from anywhere.'

I'm an alien. I'm an invasive giant bacteria from the language warp.

Well, not exactly . . . I'm more easily categorisable than that by far. Truth is, I'm a mid-sized, irreplaceable language guard. My accent and I epitomise America's mid-Pacific future. I am [Newspaper]'s quantum of Australianness. The foreignness and yet localisation embodied in me co-exist in a mid-Pacific whirl of conflict and potential conflict. There is no point pretending otherwise. I am centrally marginal and marginally central.

I have 'perspective'—that's what I wrote on the [Newspaper] employment application form all those years ago—and 'empathy', which I emphasised in the subsequent interview. I could bring your newspaper (or, as I implied in that interview, your 'culture') depth and nonetheless retain its historical uniqueness. With a few simple linguistic twists, I can increase your newspaper's reach without loyal, years-long customers even noticing the influx of other-cultural interests into the reading neighbourhood. If I can sell me to you, I can sell your—or should I say 'our'?—newspapers to millions more Americans and new Americans. People will want to immigrate just to have the daily deliveries, I assure you of that. And all on a sub-editor's salary! Amazing. Sure I'm confident, perhaps too confident. But as you may know, confidence is a cultural thing. I'm not yet sure of the appropriate confidence level to project in US employment interviews at major newspapers. On the other hand, you can bet that I'm the only interview subject who even thought it was an issue, let alone one that could add shade to your award-winning news stories. All of which could bring in readers previously put off by their discomfort with current news-confidence projections. Believe me. In fact, I'll give you my personal guarantee. Tell you what, I'll work the first two weeks for half-price. You won't do better than that. My accent might be floating, but it is in very, very warm water.

Or something like that. I didn't show any slides, or play a tape of lapping water, and I can't remember all the exact words. I was offered the job immediately, my Australian references unverified and unverifiable (the newspaper which allegedly employed me over there had folded six months earlier).

Now, this feeds straight into Dida's and my discussion about the police. We have a hat (Australian) and a bow tie (distinctly, uniquely, Steve's). The guy is missing, and underdressed. We strongly suspect a crime may have been committed. We have evidence which may be crucial to the location of Steve and any abductor. We have only a few leads to follow (names and phone numbers Bea gave Dida), no resources (like a finger-print flickbook or flashcards illustrating chin-types) and no expertise in hunting down suspects. We have a lightbulb's chance in space of illuminating the mystery word puzzle in yesterday's [Newspaper], let alone solving a disappearance. We're hopeless. Perhaps, after all, we should let the cops know what we know.

'So,' says Dida, 'you wanna go to the police? Just because we've got two pieces of peripheral clothing instead of one?'

'I didn't say I wanted to,' I say. I simultaneously want to and want not to. I want Steve to be found and alive, but I don't want to speak to the police. I want no longer to be responsible for the pieces of evidence we have discovered, but I don't want to hand them over to the police to bag and file and, after a statutory period, lose. I want the full resources of the police department to be brought to bear on this particular disappearance, but not on coincidental discoveries related to the contents of my apartment, which is full of equipment engraved with 'This item has been stolen from [Newspaper]. Any information leading to its recovery will be rewarded richly.'

I have a company memo pinned to the company noticeboard above the company computer which sits on the company desk in front of the company chair in my little office in the corner of the room. The memo warns of dire consequences for employees who use company equipment for non-company business. Beside it, I've pinned another letter which says (in part):

Owing to the sudden termination of your employment, you are required to return all [Newspaper] property within forty-eight (48) hours.

My reply is tacked up beside it, as a kind of intra-apartmental taunt:

To the Property Manager:

Please note I have never taken any [Newspaper] property outside the company limits.

Yours faithfully,
Vernon Collins.

'I've had police experiences too,' Dida tells me. Lots of egg-throwing and tomato-throwing. Incidences of screaming and chaining to mayoral gates. Etc.

The police, we decide with reluctance and relief, can wait a while. They're trained to be patient. I once rewrote a story which said, in part, before I changed its emphasis, 'Specialised police units can hold sieges and continue negotiations for many days or even weeks, where necessary.'

After my attentions, the story purported to quote an anonymous high-ranking police officer worrying that, 'Police no longer know how to close an incident.'

CHAPTER 3

Justice Department of the State of New York
Post Office Box 1111, Central Post Office,
New York City, NY

Summons

Re: People v Vernon Collins

Mr Vernon Collins is ordered to appear at
Manhattan Central Court,
182 Avenue of the Americas,
in its criminal jurisdiction at
9.30 a.m./p.m. on 14 November 199_ to answer
three counts of wrongful appropriation
one count of grand-theft.

Mr Vernon Collins is advised that, should he be
unable to procure appropriate legal representation due to impecunity, an Attorney will be
appointed by the Court.

Mr Vernon Collins is further advised that he will
be advised in the event of any alteration of the
charges or postponement of the hearing. Should

Mr Vernon Collins obtain an Attorney prior to
the hearing, he should advise Mr Nicholson S.
Grant Senior, 3rd Assistant Deputy Vice-Secretary
of the Justice Department, on 212 JUSTICE/fax
212 333 FINE. Mr Grant will ensure that appropriate and timely information is provided to Mr
Vernon Collins' Attorney.

Mr Vernon Collins is further advised that should,
due to any foreseeable or unforeseeable circum-
stance or vicissitude, he be unable to attend the
designated Court at the designated time (see
above), he should advise Mr Nicholson S. Grant
Snr, 3rd Assistant Deputy Vice-Secretary of the
Justice Department, on 212 JUSTICE/fax 212
333 FINE. Failure to do so could result in arrest
and/or the imposition of onerous bail conditions.

Yours sincerely,
Nicholson S. Grant Senior (Mr)
3rd Assistant Deputy Vice-Secretary
Justice Department of the State of New York

For a few minutes I say, 'Fuckfuckfuckfuckfuckfuck
fuckfuckfuckfuckfuckfuckfuckfuckfuckfuckfuckfuck
fuckfuckfuckfuckfuckfuckfuckfuckfuckfuckfuckfuck
fuckfuckfuckfuckfuckfuck,' and Dida keeps trying to
have me explain, asking, 'What? What? What? What?
What? What?' now and then between my syllables.
Muffy starts barking, perhaps believing the room has
filled with chicken impersonators.

'Fucking Eisenhower,' I tell Dida eventually. Or I say
'Fucking Eisenhower' around the room and Dida
assumes I'm talking to her. 'This is typical of him. This
is exactly what he would do.

Eisie was always on about how we got sued by
every 'wronged' lowlife criminal in the city and if he
had his chance he'd litigate fucking litigate until the

entire court system was clogged with cases brought by [Newspaper].

'That'd teach the fuckers,' he'd grumble to in-favour staffers—of whom, more than apparently, I am one no longer.

'So,' says Dida, gesturing at my workspace, 'what are you going to do? Give all this crap back?'

'No way,' I say. 'I'm going to get myself the smooth-est lawyer in town, and countersue for harassment, breach of privacy and assault. Anything else I think of, too. I am very ready for this game. You know who that lawyer is?'

'Not hard to guess. Harry X. Pewley?'

'Exactly.'

'I like the idea of that after all,' Dida says. 'You having bullshitted your cute, unqualified, imaginary way into some imaginary big-shot law firm.'

'Yeah,' I say. 'That's what I've done.'

Muffy whines because we take more than twenty-five seconds from the mention of the word 'walk' until we leave. The poor little dog.

'OK, Muffy, come on! We're going already,' Dida and I tell him. He stops whining and starts barking. Recently, Muffy has taken to voicing his displeasure with all things newspapery. He seizes sheets of news-paper from the streets and shakes them to pieces, he urinates on the dispensers and barks at the street vendors. I have unconsciously communicated to him that [Newspaper] is the enemy, and Muffy is fiercely, inimitably, caninely loyal. Some days, he hardly lets us read the newspapers before he shreds them. He is an excellent and persistent shredder. Muffy is a bril-liant little dog, intellectually head and shoulders above all of his species. Once, he was shredding a sheet of newspaper, urinating on a dispenser, and barking, all at the same time. Dida begins to call him President Dog, but stops when he repeatedly ignores her, no doubt judging her anthroposociocentric.

'Too American,' I tell her. 'Muffy's a mid-Pacific dawg. Muffy and I are very close, culturally.'

'Yeah, yeah,' she grumbles.

She goes back to calling him Muffy, and he wags his stubby little white tail and barks enthusiastically.

On this walk, we stop at a newspaper vendor and I buy [Newspaper]. Muffy is very angry, growling and barking, and Dida has to restrain him by hanging onto his collar. He pulls against the collar very hard and almost stops breathing, so he has to relax. Then he coughs a couple of times and barks some more.

'Wouldn't like to meet that dog in a alleyway,' the vendor tells me. 'He sounds real mean for a little feller.'

'He is,' I say. 'Aren't you, Muffy?'

Muffy barks.

Muffy: *Dust is like atmospheric art, temporary drawings on the sky. Dust is how you know where the air is and where the wind is going, even if, on a physical level, you know already, because it has gone into your eyes. Dust sometimes moves with the traffic, stopping at the stoplights and giving way to pedestrians and people on bicycles and purveyors of apples and pears pushing carts of produce. Dust is something you can never catch because once you have caught it, it's no longer dust. It's grime or dirt or feathers. Dust is the roads getting enthusiastic. It is the meaning of 'carried away'. Dust is always carried away. It is easy to be enthusiastic about dust. Sometimes there are huge pieces of dust which you catch and then they turn out to be cardboard boxes. Tiny pieces hide in nostrils all over the city. We could have a giant dust hunt and everyone would find as much as he or she wanted.*

[Newspaper] is not yet giving up on me. Although I like to believe I can outlast it for waiting and patience, it has the advantage of being a corporate entity with unlimited resources and which never sleeps or eats, whereas I am handicapped by being an ex-employee.

Today's special surprise is a neat, well-designed advertisement—a 3x2 inch duotone—in a prominent position on an odd-numbered news page. 'Where is Steve?' it asks, and the accompanying graphic depicts an Australian-style panama hat. I feel myself becoming pale. I sit down. What is this advertisement doing in [Newspaper]? What does [Newspaper] know of Steve's disappearance or of the hat in my apartment? Who could place such an ad? Could this be aimed at me?

'What the fuck?' I whisper.

Dida has a filing system with a file labelled 'Steve'. I believe this file includes all the notes from her meetings with Steve's friends and family. I say 'I believe' because I have not seen it.

'I could practically write his biography already,' she boasts. 'I have all the information on his birthplace, childhood, family, personal heroes, education.'

When I ask for a squizz, my loving girlfriend tells me to go ride a carrot. Since I walked out on our interview with Bea, Dida has been informationally circumspect. I even attempt humility: 'You were so right and I was wronger than wrong' etc., but she's not buying.

'I'm not buying, but I might trade,' she says, partially bending to my 'but we're a team' argument. 'Might. You find out who placed that ad, or whether it was an in-house job, and then we'll see.'

I'm convinced. I dial.

'Good afternoon, [Newspaper],' says a voice.

'Classified advertising, please.'

'Placement or complaints, sir?'

'Management office, thank you.'

'Thank *you*. Putting you through.'

'Hello. You have reached the office of Peter Janowski, manager of classified advertising. I am away from my desk at the moment, but will be back shortly. Your custom means a lot to me. Please leave a message and I will be happy to return your call.'

Shit. Leave a message or not? What if someone else gets it? It could be trouble for Pete. I'd have to state clearly that there hasn't been regular contact between us and that I'm initiating. But then they might think I'm getting desperate. But who are 'they', anyway, and why would they give a flying fuck about my contact with Pete? But, but, but . . . When the voicebox of the panicked man is forced to operate, it can produce inspired words: 'Pete? You there? Pete? Pete? It's me, Eugene. You remember? I'll call you at 6.11 p.m.'

'Good evening, [Newspaper].'

'Classified advertising, management office, thank you.'

'Thank *you*. Putting you through.'

'Hello. You have reached the office of Peter Janowski, manager of classified advertising. I am away from my desk at the moment, but will be back shortly. You custom means a lot to me. Please leave a message and I will be happy to return you call.'

'Pete? Pete?'

Click. 'Hello.'

'It's Vernon.'

'Oh, for Chrissake. What's with all the bullshit?'

'Sorry. I didn't want to talk to anyone else. I am seriously erased from the good books.'

'I heard. What do you want from me?'

'A medium-sized favour.'

'Come on, Vern. You're out of here.'

'Be nice. Remember your Sydney holiday.' (I'd convinced management that Sydney newspapers ran far more efficient classifieds than we did, and that sending Pete to fact-find would be extremely advantageous.)

'OK, OK. What do you fucking want, nice?'

'I need to know who placed an ad, page A11, mid-right.'

(The sound of pages turning.)

'That's a display ad. Wrong department.'

'Come on. Do me this favour. I don't know any of those sleazy hotheads.'

'I'll find out. I'll call you.'

'Thanks a lot. We'll be even. I mean it.'

'Don't worry about it. You fucking Australian dipshit.'

'You're a nice guy.'

'Yeah. Fuck off.' Click.

The melted-down routine of my life is setting into gelatinous regularity. Regular fucking, eating, walking and managing of ever-multiplying crises. Regular social life: me, Dida, Muffy. Regular harassment from my ex-colleagues. Regular trailing around after Dida as she pretends competence in missing persons location. Regular regular regular. I wonder if this is what it means for a life to 'turn out'. Have I 'ended up'? Even these thoughts, I realise, are cyclic. I remember thinking the same things in Australia. I ended up working very briefly in the insurance industry. I turned out OK: I had friends, a lover, regularity. Then I tossed in that life and reinvented myself in America. I swapped Australian spring for New York fall, October 1983. Was this move the start of a new cycle? Was I rebirthing myself into an American, slowly acculturating? If the city remade the person . . .

Aaargh, what if I've done the wrong thing, tossing in my job and staying around New York? At least I could have changed my name to something interesting and untraceable, or moved over to Jersey. Vladimir Stoltz, MD. Sounds okay, I suppose. Professor Richard Wansborough, David Mamet IV, Hieronymus Ng. I'm tempted to become Harry X. Pewley permanently, to spend my life harassing the harassers with irritating correspondence. *This* would be a project for a contemporary Robin Hood.

Dida compensates for everything. Being with her. Even when she's organised. I love the way her breast size changes, up and down, following the cycles of the moon. She is constantly in flux, constantly remaking herself. Sometimes she is the detective, sometimes the lover; sometimes she is Muffy's managing director, taking sole responsibility for his exercise and feeding cycles. I am with Dida in all her manifold phases.

'Tell me all your secrets,' I whisper to her one night.

She mumbles, 'Mmm mm mmmm nn.'

In the morning I say, 'You told me all your secrets in the night.'

'What were they?' she demands. I am forced to admit that, while I heard clearly what she said, I couldn't understand a syllable.

Dida and I discover we enjoy dancing, but are more skilled in its parody than its actuality. Similarly with synchronised swimming. Synchronised swimming seems to be about moving through a succession of poses as if being photographed. Adapting this sport for the bedroom produces a staccato fuck-effect, with lots of accompanying mutual praise: 'Ta-dum!' or 'A very fine pike indeed.'

Newspapers suck information in, mulch it into generic shape, and expel it into the world. Their organisational culture is highly evolved to facilitate this process. I am not surprised that Pete calls back very soon.

'I found out what you wanted.'

'That's great, Pete. What's the answer?'

'I can't really pronounce it.'

'You can't pronounce the person who placed the ad? They're Eastern European, for example?'

'Corporation, Vern. Not a person. And there's nothing to pronounce. That's the whole problem. It's, like, an asterisk. Asterisk Inc. Or maybe it's not said like that, not said at all. It's just written asterisk, capital-I-n-c.'

'No other information? An address?'

'That's it. Look, I told you. It's not my department. It's Display.'

'That's OK. You're a genius. That's fantastic. Can you e-mail or fax it to me, so I can see it? I really appreciate it, Pete. I really do.'

'Sure you do. I'll send it from a public fax down the road. I'm not getting caught with your number in here, buddy. Now we're even, OK? So leave me alone.'

'Sure, Pete.'

'Fuck off.' Click.

Good news. There *are* solutions to problems.

Although I am not constipated, I remember the slogan of a prominent Australian breakfast cereal manufacturer: 'Dream Believe *Create* Succeed'.

The fax arrives. I show Dida the information. She is impressed.

'I didn't know you had contacts who would actually come through,' she tells me.

'Now can I look at "Steve"?'

'In a little while.' She tugs at my buttons which, as she knows they will, come apart in her hands.

* is not listed on Wall Street. The Dow Jones Industrial Average pays no heed to it, at least not knowingly. * is not in the telephone book. Dida looks in telephone books with pages of every colour and never finds a listing for *. I suggest we cannot be sure where in the alphabet * occurs, so we need to check at the beginning and end of every letter's entry in the telephone book. Dida says, 'That's totally ridiculous, Vern,' but does it anyway. I know it's ridiculous, too, but I double-check. We find nothing—except if we include a minor disagreement over whether we have conducted twenty-seven or fifty-two searches. I say it's twenty-seven, because the end of 'A' and beginning of 'B' constitute the one search, so twenty-six beginnings plus the end of zee. Dida claims we necessarily take a different search attitude with each new letter, enough to distinguish one search from another: 'You read the end of "A" in a totally different manner from the beginning of "B". Your eyes move differently about the new page. You read to the end of a letter, return to the beginning and read down. They are completely separate actions, twice per letter. So there are fifty-two.'

I maintain her approach is clumsy and lacks

panache whereas mine overflows with elegance and rightness. Outcome: unresolved. Action plan: abandon argument. I flick through the phone books of other major US cities without luck.

'It must refer to footnotes or something like that,' Dida says. For a moment we think it feasible that * is a lesser-known shoeshop, and we visit every listed footwear retailer on Manhattan. We take several days to disprove this slight idea.

Nonetheless, we have a starting point. * isn't much of a name. No one would bother about its spelling. No one has seen its letterhead. As a corporate entity, it doesn't seem to have done anything except place a single minor display advertisement to worry a former [Newspaper] employee. On the other hand, it performed this function in an extremely focused manner. It knows a few details: it has heard of Steve; it probably knows my connection with the panama hat—that is, it knows I would recognise the hat in an advertisement asking 'Where is Steve?' It may or may not know that the hat is back in my possession. It may or not have been responsible for the shift of the hat from the city to the forest. We know that it knows of the hat's connection with me. *, or *'s principals, have a link to Steve or to someone intimate with Steve. This is a strong hypothesis. No, fuck it, that has to be a fact. We know something about *.

Knowledge is a major turn-on. I can empathise with Archimedes charging nakedly and knowledgeably down the street, telling everyone within shout-range of his learning. Naturally, Dida and I celebrate our wisdom by fucking each other brainless. Later, lying there not smoking cigarettes, I say, 'And then there's your Steve file. That's something we have. You should open a * file as well.'

'I already did,' says Dida. 'And they are cross-referencing very easily.'

I'm about to ask her to show me when Muffy, that subgenius of timing, starts barking and scratching at the bedroom door. He wants a walk and he wants it now. Guess who gets his desire.

Outside, Muffy becomes much calmer. He trots up the street. He trots around the park. He urinates gracefully on lampposts and trees, lifting his leg unhurriedly, sending out a neat stream, then lowering the leg again. Approach a tree. ONE-two-three, move along li'l doggie, ONE-two-three—practically a polka. Inside, he's a complete terror: unpredictable, demanding. Outside, he is totally at ease. Trot trot, tongue tasting atmospheric variations, occasionally whining for ice cream.

Muffy: *Biscuit cracker scone*
bone bone bone
I like to eat in company
I like to eat alone.

In the United States of America, lack of income is something of a disadvantage. The human body requires a given level of nutrition to sustain itself. Dida and I are involuntarily losing weight, and the US government doesn't give a damn. They probably don't even know. We could tell them, I suppose, but that would only draw attention to ourselves and, ultimately, to our growing collection of Steve's discarded clothing.

'I don't even like to say the word, Dida,' I tell her. 'But I am going to have to find some W-O-R-K.'

'There must be some alternative, Vern,' she says.

We come up with nothing. Dida has barely enough to support herself, especially now she has been our sole earner for several weeks. Manhattan rents rank up there with the greatest, and freelance phone techs seem to spend most of their time helping friends. Also, for the moment, Dida is determined to be a detective, and the pay is never in advance, especially as she's hired herself. Muffy is incapable of going down the mines or robbing banks. It's too late to grow vegetables and become self-sufficient, besides which, tilling the carpet is specifically outlawed in my lease. I am not yet desperate enough to break and enter. The answer is work.

'Ah well, worse things have happened,' we tell each other. As a freelancer, I still wouldn't ever have to leave the apartment.

Also, by working for others, I will probably make it more difficult for [Newspaper] to claim I have an on-going and exclusive contract or employment relationship with it. I'll tell the judge I've always been freelance and that there had been an oral contract agreeing to release me from the written contract at any time on my request. The agreement was never set down in writing because Personnel would have made too much fuss and [Newspaper] needed me to start immediately. Yes. I'd believe the story myself. In exchange for this oral understanding, I agreed to start that very day—this is what I would tell the judge— provided no action was taken for breach of contract should I choose to leave. I also agreed—and Dida thinks this imaginary clause adds bucketloads of credibility—that upon quitting [Newspaper], I would not work for a major competitor for at least a year. A very likely scenario, this one. I sound reasonable. I sound honest. I sound unlike anyone who would voluntarily commit her- or himself to a lifetime's journalism.

I immediately write a backdated memo addressed

to ex-boss Eisie, setting out the terms of our 'agreement', and put it between the relevant pages of my then-current work diary.

'I cannot believe I forgot to give it to him,' I'll tell the court, 'but I guess we all forget things sometimes.'

The best thing about this particular set of lies is that it keeps me away from newspapers. Newspapers can become an obsession and, as my years at [Newspaper] show, I am susceptible to vocational obsession. I pat my computer affectionately a couple of times.

'It's you, me, Dida and Muffy from now on,' I tell it.

Dida pretends to gag.

At the very back of the top drawer of my filing cabinet, I find a list of agents for freelancers. Every journalist with a quarter of a brain must have one of these files, to pretend he or she has the possibility of leaving regular and regularly paid employment for a life of free adventure and glory.

The minute I turn on my computer, which beeps familiarly and flashes 'Hello Vern! from everyone at Information Services', Muffy begins to sulk. He paces and scratches and moves from position to position, punctuating every shift with a stage-whispered whimper.

'For Chrissake, Muffy, I'm only trying to update my CV!' I snap, trying not to shout, but Muffy growls and bares his teeth. Every time I go to touch the keyboard, Muffy finds some new way to complain. He is an extremely versatile doglet. I try closing him out, but I feel too guilty and, also, I can hear him digging up the carpet, which, as I have said, is not allowed.

'You're nice to Dida,' I tell him. 'Why can't you be friends with the computer, too?'

Dida is watching with a combination of amusement and concern.

'It's not funny at all,' I say. 'Concern alone is what is called for here.'

'Think,' she says. 'The solution is no further away than your keyboard.'

I think and think and plead and plead. 'Just tell, go on, go on, pleeeeease.'

Dida refuses.

'It's *your* computer's relationship with *your* dog,' she says. 'You work it out.'

Soon after, I understand two things. First, I completely comprehend the expression 'the penny drops'. I even hear the clanking sound at the base of my skull. I think Muffy hears it too, because he looks up even before I go to get the doggie biscuits from under the kitchen sink.

Second, I know what to do: 'Muffymuffymuffy! Here dogdogdoggie! C'mon! C'mon! Look what this nice old computer has got for you, here it is, holding it on its keyboard. It's a yummyyummy dog biscuit, isn't it? Yes it is! And now the nice computer is tossing you the yummy biscuit. Whee! Isn't that delicious! What a very nice machine!'

The retraining exercise takes four days, and succeeds. Muffy gains a new best friend, and an old computer has learnt a new trick.

My CV details a broader range of editing expertise than that of anyone I have ever met. It is possibly the most extensive in the US. One can never be too experienced for freelance work. If I were applying for full-time or permanent part-time positions, my CV wouldn't contain a quarter of this stuff. I'd be over-qualified. But it's about right for freelance. I toss up whether to have worked for Encyclopaedia Britannica, finally deciding against: one major corporation chasing me is enough. Instead of Britannica, I invent the Encyclopaedia of Eastern Australia, at which august and renowned institution I suddenly have six months' exhouse fact-checking experience. I may not have too much genuine freelance experience, but I can honestly take any position requiring a sharp, business-relevant imagination.

I send copies to the agencies second-, third- and fourth-nearest the apartment. Applying to the closest one might demonstrate sloth. The second-nearest, blandly (and inaccurately) named Westside Editing Services, telephones almost immediately. The agent's name is Sarah Kadaré, and she's got work right now. Do I want it? The pay's good, and she doesn't need to meet me because she is so impressed with my CV, though of course she would love to meet very soon, but now she'll just e-mail the job straight to me, and how do I wish to be paid, the pay on this one is not as high as some, but it's the first job after all, and the client is a regular so she's sure there'll be no problem with increasing the payment second time around and of course she's very sure there will be more, so not to worry, but is it adequate for a start, she's sure it is, and she can arrange direct deposit or courier me the cheque as soon as she receives it herself, minus fifteen per cent, which might be more than many, but it's less than some others and she bears most expenses herself, so there's nothing more to pay.

I decide I do want the job, which is for some magazine whose name she is not too sure how to pronounce or, in fact, she's not too sure what the name is, as with design mags it can be difficult to distinguish between text and design elements as she's sure I know, me having such broad-ranging magazine experience, and she didn't even know some of these magazines had Australian editions, isn't that interesting, anyway must go, you'll have the manuscript in ten minutes max, bye-bye, we really must try to meet very soon, and who was your Australian agent, because she might know one or two down there, or somewhere south, anyway.

'That was in the top-ten easiest scams, for certain,' I tell Dida.

'I knew I could rely on you to be a good, solid, working man,' she replies.

'You have new mail,' announces my screen. I walk around the apartment saying, 'What am I bid to end my liberty? What am I bid, ladies and little dawgs? Fivteen hundert. Fivteen hundert minus fivteen per cent. Do I hear more? I do not. Fivteen hundert going once-a. It's going twice-a.' I approach my computer and open the document. 'It's gone!'

Dida laughs and Muffy, guess what, barks. I practically bark too—Muffy starts and his fur stands up—when I see the name at the top of my screen. It's *.

Muffy: *Look up there, in mid-air, travelling northeast at around six hundred miles per hour. Wheeeeee! That makes the easterly component around four-hundred-twenty-five miles per hour. Whoooooa!! or Wowowowow! There's no time to buy and sell at that speed. All resources must be committed to staying awake and even that is almost certainly becoming too difficult. Who the hell are you up there? Why do you take such an interest in me, that you fly right over head? Surely you can't be approaching New York. There's nothing for you down here. There's nothing to do in this place but count the hairs on the back of your nose. Stay away! Stay awayyyyy!!*

I remain silent for twenty seconds. I look out the

window, half-expecting some profound change to have occurred below. Next, I will concentrate on the contents of my computer screen. I will not look out the window for many hours. If the world wants me to observe a transformation, it will have missed its opportunity.

Dida comes over to my work space to see what I am making such a fuss about. I point to the screen. She purses her lips and frowns.

'It's hard to know which conspiracies to believe in,' she says.

'Yes,' I agree. 'From now, I'm believing in any that aren't reported by my former employer. Do you think it'll blow up on us?'

'Maybe I should take Muffy somewhere safe,' she muses, and mock-cowers behind an old copy of [Newspaper].

The computer doesn't explode, and nor do I. Instead, scrolling down reveals a glossy trade magazine.

The publication really does seem to be called *, and the main title is followed, in slightly smaller type, by the subtitle 'Urban Interstices'. It's an architecture rag dedicated to public space. One cover story is 'Why McDonnell Douglas Should Have Battery Park". The cover photo shows a flight of military jets approaching the park.

A second cover story is '[Newspaper]'s Private Public Sqare' (sic). It clearly needs a 'u' in square, and I'll have to think about whether it should be 'private public', 'public private', 'private/public', 'public–private' or some other permutation. Come to think of it, until this moment I had been unaware of any architectural quality around the [Newspaper] building at all. It is going to be a very long, boring job, I think, if the front cover needs that much work for a couple of measly puff-words.

I tell the word processor 'go to last page'. It is blank except for a little misspelt box saying 'plac [Newspaper] advertizement here'. I find myself hoping a lot of blank space has been left for ads.

OK. I try to gather myself together. This is work and I can do it, even if my employer wants to donate New York to armaments manufacturers. I used to perform an employment function and now shall do so again. Just like Arthur of Camelot: the once and future king. When the world needs him to rule, he shall be there. The world now needs me to help the military appear literate and logical: I am here. Go. Go. Nothing happens. I have not yet begun to work. I rise from the desk and make myself a coffee. I make a coffee for Dida. I pour some water into Muffy's dogbowl. Dida and I savour our coffee and Muffy lashes his tongue enthusiastically at the water, somehow managing to decrease its level at a far greater rate than could be accounted for by spillage.

I finish the coffee. Muffy finishes the water. Dida has finished and is sitting in the corner reading a book. I look across the room at the computer, the magazine's contents page lurking beneath a hopping-doggies screen-saver. I go to the computer. I sit down again. I sigh loudly.

'Half an hour and then we'll wrestle around beneath the eiderdown?' I suggest to Dida, who laughs with, I believe, some commitment to the plan.

We never make it to bed that afternoon, even though the contents page take no time. It holds just two typographical errors and a minor formatting problem. What keeps us from writhing nakedly is on the editorial page. Above the editorial, in the centre of page four, is a photograph of a smiling Steve: Steve hasn't disappeared after all. He is the editor of a magazine for militaristic architects. He stares out from the page at me. What is wrong with this photograph?

'He can see!' I yell. 'Look! Look!'

So, end of story; that's that for missing persons quests. Steve sneaks off, abandons his family and friends, hides his clothing round and about, places teasing display advertisements and, finally, reveals his new, sighted self to me. He has obviously had some kind of vision-emplacement surgery and now wants to surprise everyone he knows. The scenario is simple and has a nice ending—a reunion with the entire cast coming together on stage, talking, laughing and congratulating Steve on miraculously overcoming his disability: sightlessness to editorship in a matter of weeks. Such a glossy magazine, too. Tell us about your interest in military hardware, Steve! And what does Dida think of that theory?

'It's total bullshit. What's the address of that magazine, anyway? Let's go,' Dida huffs.

* magazine's only given address is a box number in SoHo. The three of us go there. The box is set into the wall of a small, downmarket convenience store, the type of place that sells only five varieties of milk and where the vegetables have lost all crispness. I have no idea why they're called *convenience* stores when it's much easier to phone for a pizza, but there you go. Muffy sniffs with distaste at a few sacks of past-their-use-by-date dry dogfood. The store owner or assistant loudly slaps his magazine on the service counter and calls out, 'No dogs. No dogs in here. That's the regulations. No exceptions.'

We cross the road. We didn't like that store, did we

Muffy? No no no. I think about whether dogs apprehend time in the same way as humans. For example, does Muffy already know what's about to happen? Does he know who is about to walk around the corner? If he does, why is he so calm?

Two men walk around the corner in earnest conversation. Well, they could be repeating, 'Jack Shit was a farmer,' but they seem to be listening to each other. The man on the right is Steve, having no trouble with his vision. The other man is Eisie. Steve takes a key from his pocket, opens his postal box, and takes out three or four thin envelopes. He puts them in his jacket pocket. Eisie says something else to him and then looks across the street. I'm looking at Eisie and he sees me. He says something else to Steve and they both start running across the road towards us.

'Run,' I say to Dida, and we do.

CHAPTER 4

Muffy: *Running, running. What a wonderful world this is, with all its stairways and underpasses. So many people running and so many others walking quite quickly. There are friendly people to run with and unfriendly people to run from. There are indifferent people to run around or past. Also, there are wheeled vehicles of unpredictable speed. There are innumerable large, static objects whose presence creates corners around which to run. There are slight downhill gradients where your hind legs catch your forelegs and there are slight uphill gradients where they do not. Sometimes you go so fast your ears turn inside out and sometimes you slow down and shake your head and they pop back the right way.*

New York could be taken apart and put back together so easily. The buildings and the sounds. Everywhere in the city sounds come: oh, oh, oh, oh, oh, oh from one apartment, hah! hah! hah! hah! hah! from another, ooooOOOOoooo . . . ooooOOOOoooo . . . ooooOOOOoooo . . . from over on Lafayette, hheeehheeehheeehheeeshhh up there, all adding to the vowelly-aspirative atmosphere of the great metropolis, the overall hoiaeuuioaeoiueaiouohieoiuaeheueoiuoi-

heuioueohieoiuaeoiehaueu that is this incredible city, the accumulation of people breathing in a happy, excited manner as they run with or chase after the dogs.

Steve and Eisie chase after us and we are chased by them. We flag a taxi.

'Y'unnerstan I haveta surcharge ya thirty per cent for thuh dawg,' the driver greets us. 'I'd prefer not ta, but I haveta.'

We nod rapidly. He has initiative and business nous. He unnerstans about supply and demand. This is good. He probly oughta starta newspaper.

'Go, go,' I urge him.

'Lose the creeps following,' says Dida.

'I'll do my best, lady.'

He fails, perhaps because his initiative is limited to ripping off tourists or perhaps because taxi drivers operate best with a destination in mind. If the latter is the reason, our pursuers give their driver a far easier task: 'follow that car'. Dida's Plan B is to direct randomly—left, left, left, right, straight, right, left. Eisie and Steve sit in the back seat of their cab with their wallets at the ready, feeling pretty smug as the two cars creep through the heavy Manhattan traffic. I realise it's the first time I've seen a car chase from the perspective of the chasees. We cannot escape because our role is not properly culturally delineated.

We watch them follow us two or three cars back for fifteen dollars' worth plus thirty per cent. Unless we cross to New Jersey we don't stand a chance.

'Joisey, exit three,' I tell him, trying to sound as assertive as a native New Yorker.

'I'm not drivin' no dog across no state lines. Thirty per cent or fifty per cent or nothing. I'm staying right here on this island. You decide if or when you want to finish this game and I will stop the taxi. And if your

dog makes any kind of mess there will be a cleanin'
charge of fifty dollars.'

'I understand why people always get caught in
these car chases,' I mutter to Dida, who has kept up
a rat-tat-tat of directional commands and still seems
optimistic that we will somehow evade our pursuers.
'Revert to foot?'

'Check. This'll do,' she commands. We pull up with
a slight squeal, as though the driver had been going
at pace. We've stopped outside the very department
store that provided my first New York employment
and half my household goods. Hey, I recognise this
place, I say to myself. It's been a while since my last
visit, but here I am again. How convenient, I think,
and I also think: I hope they don't remember me. I
hand the driver some notes, including an extremely
small tip.

'Keep the change. Come on, Muffy.'

We run into the store as the second cab pulls up
outside.

'This way,' I order, waving towards where the
employees' exit is or used to be. I see Eisie and Steve
pointing us out to each other. At the main entrance,
they momentarily adopt an abridged marines-hoist-
the-flag-on-Iwo-Jima pose. If only I'd remembered my
camera.

'Let's go,' I say.

We dodge between the stands of overly made-up
women selling cosmetics, the well-shod college stu-
dents in footwear, the young men and women dressed
in catalogue-perfect variations of each other in the
clothing departments. A man with an armful of shirts
snaps, 'Rude!' at me as I propel myself past him by
grabbing his coatsleeve. If I were skiing, the customers
would represent an endless supply of stocks. Dida

calls, 'Danger! Danger! Rabid dog!' to clear a path. Muffy for once is silent, concentrating on running under racks of second-rank designer suits. We're down the steps, through the code-operated door and out into the alley. They haven't changed the combination in a decade. I wonder if their insurers know.

Having escaped, however temporarily, we ought to be flushed with success. Nope. While Muffy is probably ready for another mile or two, Dida and I are wrecked. I feel like a steamroom on legs; Dida puffs and wheezes like a brass band clearing saliva from fifteen trombone u-bends. What's more, we don't know what to do next. Like, once you've run away, do you simply go home? Would that be the end of it? I'd go home and finish the editing job and then try and find some other work? Why were we running away in the first place?

'Why,' I suggest, 'don't we see what they want?'

In retrospect, I see this idea indicates a shortfall in oxygen supply to the brain, a lack which had equally affected Dida.

'Sure,' she pants. 'Whatever.'

Muffy wags his tail. This means he wants some ice cream.

Immediately, Steve and Eisie come charging around the corner.

'Hello,' I say. 'What can we do for you?'

Steve holds his hand up: a cop commanding recalcitrant teenagers to come to a complete halt. We are already standing still. I am about to explain this to him when two huge men pad around the corner towards us and another two trot up from the opposite direction.

'Ah,' I deduce, raising a finger.

'Shit,' says Dida.

The men come very close. They are smiling.

'You'll want to come with us,' Steve says, in a mid-western accent.

'Just what I was going to suggest myself,' I tell him. 'Come on, Muffy.'

One of the hoods eyes the dog dubiously.

'Don't worry, he'll behave. I think he already likes you,' I tell him.

Dida, Muffy and I are locked in the windowless rear of a delivery van with three of the men. It is a good idea if you're kidnapped to befriend your captors. They're less likely to hurt you. I read this in a book by a British former SAS major whose views [Newspaper] felt were extremely newsworthy. I had made his interview quotes sound articulate and, more challengingly, intelligent. Here goes.

'I'm Vernon,' I begin. 'This is Dida, and the cute fluffball just here is Muffy.'

No one else says anything.

'Muffy is a very nice little dog,' I say. 'A lot of people are suspicious of little dogs. You'll hear all kinds of stories about them snapping and being jealous and difficult to toilet-train and so forth, but I've found the opposite with Muffy. He is so good-natured. He loves children, too. Our neighbours have a little boy called Tony, about six or seven, and Muffy simply adores him. The boy likes the dog, too. They spend hours together in the park or tearing up and down the corridors or playing in the lifts. They're the best of companions. Sometimes kids can get a bit sick of the company of their peers, and a dog like this is ideal.'

I can hear voices in the front of the truck, but it is impossible to decipher what they're saying. The truck starts forward, backs, goes forward again. We must have pulled out of the parking spot and onto the road.

'Any of you have a dog?' I say, in the general direction of the men. One looks at me with an expression between sympathy and derision. The others don't react.

'I'm a journalist myself.'

This is apparently what you tell people who might be politically active and might prefer positive (or less negative) press coverage to criticism offset only by ransom.

'Though originally from Australia.'

Can't be too careful with political types: make sure they know you're not American.

'Sydney, a lovely city. Beaches, amusements parks, plenty of movie theatres, nice parkland, good night-life.'

I notice Dida holding her face as if she's about to unscrew her cheeks.

'I guess you guys have never been there.'

I stop talking for a few minutes.

The truck jerks suddenly to the left and stops. I hear a sound like an ocean liner cat-rubbing itself against the Statue of Liberty. I recognise that! It's the rolling-up of the metal security door over the driveway which leads into [Newspaper]'s underground carpark. The truck moves forward again slowly and tilts down a steep incline. The truck stops.

'You know,' I say, helpless against my own nervous enthusiasm, 'this is the second former workplace I've visited today.'

The largest of the three looks startled.

'Never mind about that,' he says, and then, redundantly, 'you come with us.'

The doors swing open. The goons march Dida, Muffy and me in formation towards what I know to be the centre of the building. They direct us into a huge, windowless cement room, unfurnished except for several rows of large, waist-level tables.

'This was the paste-up room when pasting up was a job,' I explain to anyone listening. 'Some time between hot type and virtuality.'

The door closes behind us and a key turns.

'We wait here,' I tell Dida.

'Yes, Vern. I already got that message.'

I hoist myself onto a lay-out bench.

'I'm really sorry about all this,' I say. 'Waiting to talk to those two men was an error of judgement.'

'They would have come for you eventually. And I would have been caught up too. So don't concern yourself about that. Concern yourself about this.'

'I will. I really will.'

This is probably the most boring room Muffy has ever been in. I've seen it all before, and Dida, as a telecoms type, is used to pure functionalism. Muffy, though, looks desperate. He runs around and around the room as if a door might appear anywhere, any time. He urinates against a couple of bench legs. He whines. He scratches at the thick, locked exit door. Nothing he attempts has any effect. He is still inside and he continues to eat nothing. I call him over and scratch behind his ears in a slow, sorry-little-doggie manner. Dida scratches behind his ears too.

'It'll be OK,' she tells him and us. 'It'll be OK.'

Muffy falls asleep.

An incalculable amount of time later, the door is unlocked and a big man brings a square box in.

'Pizza,' he says, and locks us in again.

I take a bit and am not overwhelmed by the taste of bitter almonds, nor do I experience sudden pains or dizzy sensations. I do not begin to tell truths from my childhood. I do not catch little pieces of glass in my fillings. I don't care that it's cold and flavourless: it's not a bad pizza. Dida joins in and Muffy, who has been asleep for a short time, wakes up salivating profusely and whines for the eighth of a second that lapses between his conscious interest and receiving his own slice.

Assuming we are fed at regular meal-times, our confinement lasts three nights. It is punctuated only by lavatory breaks for Dida and me. The men's room is a windowless cubicle. I sit for as long as possible, until there is a pounding on the door and a big man's voice says, 'Let's go.'

Muffy had been included in the toilet roster, but the first time a big man tries to attach a rope to lead him outside, Muffy growls and snaps at his fingers. The big man leaves and returns with a few copies of [Newspaper].

'Hope he's toilet-trained,' he says. 'Wrap it up in this. And no jokes about uses for print media.'

On the second day or, if that estimate is incorrect, between meals four and five, a big man tells us, 'EIC will see you shortly.'

Muffy says nothing. Occasionally he chooses a new quadrant of the room to explore fully, sifting over the numerable scents like an archaeologist after pottery fragments. He is methodical, and never too excited. He also proves highly skilled at evacuating on the newspaper.

Muffy: *When you've lived all your life in the one city, points of difference and change become smaller and smaller. A dog becomes skilled at noticing the tiny things. A local dog is always better at noticing than a well-travelled one, in my opinion. For example, a crack in the pavement might remain the same for months then, seemingly without cause, lengthen by a foot or even more overnight. An unseen neighbour who has always had the kindest of voices might one day lose his or her temper. People with whom the dog has always been close, people who have walked with the dog hundreds of times across the green and asphalt stretches of New York, may suddenly stay in the one room, pausing only to speak with quavering voices or to take dough-filled packets from strangers. They may develop new rituals, new patterns of address. The city may shrink to a sparse parody of itself, where there are no longer vast blocks of concrete rebounding an infinity of noise, but only miniaturised, raised platforms on which people lie whilst the dog runs around beneath.*

Between meals eight and nine I ask the big man, 'When exactly will we see EIC?'

'At about four thirty,' he says. 'That's when you're booked in.'

'Thanks. And what time is it now?'

But he's already out the door, another healthy take-out meal deposited on the nearest bench.

Muffy, meanwhile, has learnt to sing badly. He howls and whines for minutes at a time. My throat is hoarse from screaming, 'Shut up, damn dawg!' at him. Dida tries to convince him to be quiet with calm reasoning. Neither strategy is at all effective.

After meal ten, a big man wheels a video and monitor into the room while another stands by the door. The first plugs it in and presses PLAY. The out-of-focus, low-light sequence shows me packing [Newspaper] computer equipment into a sports bag and walking off screen. The screen flickers to test pattern.

'That's all, folks,' says the second big man.

'Do you like your job?' I ask him.

'Sure do,' he says. 'Terrific retirement scheme.'

Confinement completely ruins our sex life. The possibility that huge goons employed by a large media company might at any moment bust in on us makes lovemaking much less appealing or, to use Dida's word, 'unthinkable'. Our relationship strikes the low point of its previously stellar progress. If only I had completed that half-hour's editing work. If only I had thought, That guy looks a hell of a lot like Steve but he is not the same guy. Curious coincidence such as life is full of. If only I had neglected to point out the similarity to my lover. If only I had said, 'I would love to go detectiving with you but my penis refuses to leave the house.'

I quickly discover there is no advantage in voicing such thoughts to co-confinees. In my experience, small dogs pay no attention. Persons to whom one is intimately related do not find comfort in speculation. In close, windowless quarters, furthermore, making guesses concerning the weather may not bring about fruitful discourse. In my experience, abject apology is a worthy posture, though even this should not be attempted more than once every three meals. Blaming the other party tends to cause conflict. More successful time consumption results from using available materials to play simple strategy games such as chequers and kalahar. Asking companions their life stories may be beneficial, provided the companions are human. My human companion claims some meditation skills, and I am able to take up waiting time failing to change my consciousness of entrapment, and becoming uncomfortable through sitting cross-legged on a long wooden bench. If one of your companions is an affectionate little furball, sitting on the floor may result in some disturbances through the application of the canine tongue to your cheeks and neck. If I were an investigative journalist instead of a retired sub-editor, this is what I would have to report after eleven meals.

After the fourth meal of hamburger-and-fries in a row, a big man comes to the door and says, 'You're on.'

We follow him along a couple of miles of underground corridor, and two other big men follow us. We are criss-crossing.

I say, 'I actually know this part of the building reasonably well, so it would save us all some energy if you took us straight to wherever we're going.'

'Are you Australian?' the first man asks, and turns 180 degrees so that we retrace our steps for several hundred yards, then turns around and does the same again. The two hoods following laugh roughly and, in that companionable tough-guy manner, falsely. I decide against recommending good places to visit along the north coast of Queensland. Let them waste their money in Surfers Paradise.

We are led into a lift, which, surprisingly, takes us deeper underground. The lift opens onto a huge office, plushly carpeted. There are windows all around, looking out onto backlit views of New York from the air, from the Empire State, from the Chrysler Building, from each tower of the World Trade Centre. EIC is sitting behind a desk in the centre of the room. He gestures with his chin, and the big men direct us to stand in front of his desk.

'Nice outlook from here,' I say, 'and no chance of sunburn.'

Dida nudges me to be quiet.

'So, you were in SoHo the other afternoon,' EIC says.

'Yes, and you?' I reply. 'You like SoHo?'

EIC ignores my question. 'Why were you there?'

'Hoping to meet a friend?' I suggest.

'Nope. Wrong answer,' says EIC, with a smile at the

big men. 'Have another guess. What were you doing in SoHo?'

I try the subdued approach.

'I got the address from a magazine,' I reply, quietly.

'Magazine?'

'Asterisk architecture magazine. I was editing it, as you probably know.'

'You got that job? My God. That is unbelievable. That explains it. For a few days there I thought you had talent.'

'You're claiming that wasn't a set-up?'

'I can't believe you got that job. I cannot believe it.'

I'm beginning to believe his surprise.

'And I wanted to see how Steve was getting on,' I continue, as we seem to have achieved a level of non-coercive communication.

'We'd like to leave now,' Dida adds, 'if that's OK.'

'Yes. Well, having cleared that up, you can leave pronto. My pleasure.

'First, though, a couple of minor administrative matters. The gentleman you have been mistakenly pursuing is someone whom you have never seen except in an editor's photograph. He's not the guy you think he is. He's just someone who looks a little similar. This is a big city, and many people in it look similar to other people. Also, it's best if you show no further interest in that company with the typographic symbol for a name, or its magazine.'

We very quickly agree.

'Just an anonymous editing job to me,' I say. 'I didn't even want to do it.'

He nods.

'It really shouldn't have gone to you. And with your continuing ties to this organisation, I'm very sorry you took it.'

He narrows his eyes, thinking. 'Still, you've started the job, so you may as well continue. I have the utmost confidence in your editing skills. Forget about the magazine after you've finished it. That's the solution.'

'What about the "Where is Steve?" ad? Can I ask you that?' I begin again.

'I don't know what you're talking about. This is a very large organisation. I simply have no way of keeping up with every classified or display ad placed.'

He pauses, pretending to continue to think. When he carries on, there is an added, empathetic softness in his voice, something that would sound, were he not the editor of a major daily newspaper, very similar to sincerity. 'There is one other matter I'd like to raise before you go. Vernon, I know you have your personal reasons for leaving our company, but we would be delighted to have you back on board. Consider it.'

He smiles a rich-man smile—creases from the corners of the eyes and the hint of expensive restaurant meals in the plumpness of the lips. 'If you fulfil your contract, we won't drag you through the courts for breach, either.'

'I'll think about it. I truly will,' I tell him. 'It sounds like a terrific and most understanding offer.'

He nods, and for a millisecond I believe I've convinced him that I too am a newspaperman of sincerity, but then I realise his nod is directed at the muscle. The big men make sure we're outside the building within forty-five seconds.

'I'm glad that's all over,' I tell Dida. Muffy barks at the specks of pollen catching the last of the sun. We return to our apartment, loosening our clothes on the way up in the lift to save time.

Lying in our bed, we decide that kidnapping can really interfere with people's lifestyles.

'Something to be avoided in future,' I mumble to Dida's neck, and she mumbles her concurrence.

After the anti-climatic ordeal of our appointment with the Editor in Chief, it is even more difficult to concentrate on editing Steve's magazine. I think about going back to my old job.

'Why shouldn't I?' I ask myself. 'Just because someone chases and kidnaps you, harasses you and seems to be at the root of an extremely suspicious mystery is no reason not to consider a perfectly remunerative career opportunity, a genuine second chance at the same job, if you will.'

The logic of the return to work becomes more and more appealing. I begin to picture myself on the subway in the mornings, shoulder-to-shoulder with like-minded New York citizens, all on our way to be valued and remunerated by superiors who respect our judgement and ability. Had not EIC beamed at me, implied I was indispensable? He'd practically begged me to return. He'd indicated that the distribution of power would be altered in my favour were I to return. He seemed to feel paternalistic towards me. I could tell from his eyes that he was acting in my best interests. Or, if that might have been going a little far, at least that he felt our better interests coincided. I'd have a responsible role. Things would improve. Life would go back to the way it was before I left work, excepting that Dida and I would continue to spend many, many hours together and we would share the joys of and responsibility for the warm snowball with the wet nose.

'Maybe I should return to work,' I muse to Dida.

'Loving your captors is perfectly understandable, and exhaustively classified and researched, but is not a good idea,' Dida says. 'Stockholm Syndrome, the symptoms are clear.'

As soon as she says the name, I realise how right she is. I do feel a strong affection for those big men, for EIC's smarmy mode of address, even for the abandoned lay-out tables. I had anticipated the lack of decision-making with pleasure, the dependability on muscle and smarm. Phew, I think, that was close. I was nearly a goner that time.

Dida further diagnoses that my problem is complicated, its symptoms exacerbated, because the case of the missing Steve and the found hat remains unresolved. I can't even finish the job at hand.

'How can you expect to approach the magazine's words if you don't know who has written them and in what state of consciousness?' she declares. 'I'm sure that a further day of surveillance would make the job possible.'

I'd prefer to leave the magazine unfinished, but my savings are gone—[Newspaper] never did come through with severance pay—and incoming bills these days are headed 'Third and Final Notice' or 'Notice of Intention to Disconnect'. I allow Dida to talk me into more stupidity, despite our recent kidnapping pact.

'Don't let them see us this time,' she says. At precisely this moment, Muffy indicates he wants to go for a walk. In his insistent, doggish manner, Muffy forces the issue. This dog is obviously way too qualified for dogdom. He ought to head a large retail corporation. Shouldn't you, you over-aged puppeety? Yes, bark-bark. That's what you claim now.

Back near Steve's postal box, we find well-hidden observation points behind two large trees. Muffy cannot choose between Dida and me, and skips back and forth for a few minutes before sinking to the ground, exhausted, in a sunny spot in the middle. Steve shows up, on his own this time, collects a small bundle of envelopes and heads off in the direction from which he arrived. Muffy stands up and wags his tail, adopting the I'm-about-to-bark posture. Don't do it, I pray under my breath. He doesn't verbalise a single whinette. I dare not think about cause and effect in relation to my wish and Muffy's silence. Dida and I make eye contact, she gives a brief nod towards me, and begins to sneak after Steve. I follow her. Muffy follows me for thirty seconds, then runs ahead. Steve has gone, weaving through nameless back alleys. Dida and I trot after the dawg.

At no time did I teach Muffy this newly apparent bloodhound skill. When he and I met up, I did not inquire as to his tracking ability. I thought, What a nice little pup. I will invite him to live with me. Friendship, I thought. I did not think, One day, oh seemingly talentless little fluff-in-the-box, you will be extremely useful. But only a few years later, here he is, putting me so much further in his debt.

'What a dog!' Dida mouths. I grin smugly.

Muffy: *There are ten million human paths in this city, some regular, some irregular. Some follow the one street for miles soon after sun-up, pause for several hours and then retrace the steps just before or after sundown. Some weave across and across, always choosing new, intermediate destinations. Humans move their legs up and down and wheels spin beneath them and their scent is rubber (which imprints on the ground) and perspiration, which disperses through the rich, verdant air. Now and then they temporarily abandon the wheels, run into a building, drop purposeless bundles of paper, run out, and take up wheels again. Voices crackle and break at their hips, and any canine growl causes not a jump but a swerve.*

This could be the manner in which the human species splits, that crucial evolutionary moment when those who move in straight lines at regular intervals carry on, and those who cut and change, who respond to other stimuli, who are irregular and unpredictable, who move with purposeful manner but indiscernible goals, the moment when this group takes on other, vitally distinctive attributes. They might, for example, draw nutrition from the fumes through which they pedal open-mouthed, shifting back and forth across this island like whales after plankton. They might develop to the point where motion is literally vital: any pause will cause the pulse to cease, the heart to seize up, the guts to clag out, the brain to petrify. At every moment the pedallers threaten speciation.

A dog, on the other hand, is a fixed chromosomal entity. Anyone can depend on a dog. A dog will arrive at the closed entrance and request its opening. A dog will arrive at the hour of appetite and petition relief. When a dog salivates, take it as read that salivation is the appropriate response in the circumstances.

From the change in the quality of the trash littering the sidewalks, I gauge that we have entered the financial district. It is not the brands or food quality that is distinguishable, but the ostentation of disposal. In other areas, people surreptitiously kick their discards into the gutters. Here, though, people have a right to drop it wherever it is most convenient. In this city sector, people go to 7.30 a.m. team meetings to reinforce their claims to such rights. At these meetings they affirm: 'Yes! With confidence we can move forward! Let us not deviate! Let us stride down the centre of the pavement! Let us not give way to the traffic!'

This attitude is apparent. We step carefully so as not to slip on the smears of fastfood.

Muffy leads us to the ugliest building I have seen

in all the years I've been in Manhattan. Could this twenty-storey pile of rust and appalling yellow brick be the headquarters of an architectural magazine? At any moment it will collapse. Muffy scratches at a steel door between two rusted Corinthian columns. We push at it and it creaks open. We are in a long grey corridor. Ambience: lunatic asylum *c*.1890. A hacked-up, double-doored lift is to one side. The lights above it indicate the lift is parked on the twentieth floor. Ah-ha.

'We'll come back when he's gone,' Dida says firmly.

'Good idea. By the way, I had this whole method worked out for determining which floor he was on, had these indicator lights been absent or malfunctioning. We'd press the button and see how long it took to get here. Then we'd just catch the lift up to the tenth floor, time it down—I mean, it could go slower on the way up than down, that's why you always have to time it on the way down. If it took longer than the first time, catch it again to the fifth, or if shorter, to the fifteenth, and so forth.'

'Very good,' says Dida, for some reason rolling her eyes. 'Let's go get a drink. You talking always makes me thirsty.'

'That's two good ideas, Dida. I sure do have a positive effect on you. Come on, Muffy.'

There is a small, dimly lit winebar across the road from Steve's building. It is so dark, in fact, that when Muffy sits under the table the barman cannot see him to toss him out. Stay, doggito. I ask the barman for Australian wine.

'We got some of that somewhere,' he says, with a slightly dubious expression. 'Here we go, "Koala Juice Claret". Wouldn't drink it myself, but then I'm not blessed with your accent. A glass of that for you and something more palatable for your friend?'

'Make it two beers,' I tell him.

'Good idea.'

'And a jug of water.'

'No problem.'

I pay him and return to our table, then put the water jug on the floor whereupon Muffy helps me breach New York Health Ordinance Number __: prohibition on the use of human tableware for feeding of animals.

While I am doing this contemporary hunter-gatherer thing, Dida spies on the entrance to Steve's building. I've hardly managed to smear foam around my mouth before Dida calls out, 'Bingo!'

We wait long enough to make sure Steve doesn't return, and also to finish a third round of beers.

'I guess there's not much point one of us keeping watch,' Dida says as we recross the road, 'seeing as how you'd have no way of warning me even if someone was coming.'

'You don't have a couple of those mobiles with you?'

'Only one.'

'Oh well, I knew the telephone would never replace the walkie-talkie. Besides, other people's offices fascinate me.'

Actually, I hate offices and cannot remember why I agreed to follow Steve this second time after the pointed lesson of our first attempt. The beer has gone to my head. Sometimes I can drink a barrel of the stuff and nothing. Sometimes, a sniff of the ringpull and I'm flying. This time is of type two.

The steel door is still unlocked. The lift smells strongly of urine, reminding me of the volume of beer consumed. I need to take a leak myself, but think what a poor example it would set my dog. The lift proceeds with little speed and tremendous jerks to the twentieth floor, as if someone were hauling it hand over hand. There, we find ourselves in another long, dark corridor.

'That way,' Dida decides, arbitrarily. She has chosen wisely. We encounter a door with * carved into the woodwork.

'Bullseye,' I say.

'Well, mm,' she says. 'Lend me a credit card.'

She works it between the door and its frame. One more tap and we're inside. Another amazing skill: I'm suddenly accompanied by Wondernose and Daughter of Houdini.

'So much for security,' she says. 'I thought your magazine had something to do with the military.'

I shrug. We are in an extremely large, poorly lit room. A few tatters of stained wallpaper boast the greatest achievements of rising damp. Against the far wall is a single table with some antique-looking instrument in the centre. On the wall, a fake bronze plaque bears the inscription 'Nothing Exceeds Like Excess'. The only chair is next to the table. On the floor beside the chair: a pile of old copies of [Newspaper], more yellow towards the bottom. I rock from foot to foot, wondering how long before we get caught.

'It's a weird sewing machine,' I whisper, indicating the antique.

'Why are you whispering?' she asks at normal volume, her voice booming and echoing around the room for about an hour. I feel hung over, even though I haven't yet slept. Muffy suddenly barks, and I believe I am being run over by a train. No one is here, however, nor any mass transit vehicles.

'Anyway,' Dida continues, slightly softer this time.

Perhaps she senses my frayed nerves need overlocking? She eliminates that possibility: 'It's not a sewing machine. It's for telegraphy. It's an antiquated transmitter. The question is, what signals is Steve sending and to whom?'

Wires from the telegraph lead to what looks like an Australian Hill's Hoist clothesline, but in miniature, and part of some kind of crane mechanism.

'This is an entirely different aesthetic to that portrayed in the magazine,' I lecture. 'This machine celebrates the modern not as a soulless, capital-driven corporate expression, but as the personified industrial entity in dynamic relation with the human spirit.'

'Interesting,' says Dida. She could have argued that we were in the engine room of ascetic corporatism, the dirty, hidden, labour-intensive back room for which the seemingly linear essences of corporate postmodernism are but a front. She doesn't. She could have made the point that it is from rooms like this that the feral drives of multinationalism and globalised media translate into an appearance of respectability and order, that this is the room where the plotting takes place. She says nothing.

Dida is examining the transmitter's wiring, crawling around it, studying it from all possible angles, lying on her back and gazing up through its centre, checking out the joins, screws, loops and whatever the proper techo terms are for the rest of the device.

'Do we know what it's for?' I ask.

'We soon will,' says Dida. 'I ought to be able to rig up a basic receiver for this redundant technology.'

I believe her. I've seen Dida's bound PhD thesis. The title is 'Reception and Amplification of Periodic Quasi-Soliton Arrangements for Personal and Semi-Personal Telecommunications Systems'.

'Dida, if I didn't already know everything about you, you'd be full of surprises. I was convinced you'd given up telecoms to become a detective, but now I rediscover you as a telecommunications engineer.'

'Yes, yes. Let's get out of here.'

'Arf.' (Muffy.)

After her re-emergence as a science butterfly from the cocoon of our love, I torture our conversations with telecommunicative metaphors, as in: 'See this breakfast cereal? Now that's what I call optical fibres. See it, eat it. Mmm it's good.'

She accuses me of having 'synchronously pumped jitter amplification' and of being 'an intercontinental pulse hampered by narrow bandwidth capabilities'.

I respond by picking up cassettes and books and computer discs and shoes and table lamps and dinner plates and shaving mirrors and bananas and screwdrivers and so on, looking intently at each, bringing it to my mouth and saying, 'Hello? Hello?'

'You need serious phase conjugation,' she tells me.

Dida is confident about her bugging abilities, but building a receiver still takes her several days. First she has to read through every essay and assignment she ever submitted, especially those of no particular relevance. Second, she has to discover that none of them is to the point and that she needs library books. Third, she has to rejoin the Society of Telecommunications Engineers library and wait for a card to arrive in the mail. Fourth, she has to borrow a soldering instrument from a former AT&T colleague (whose name I've forgotten but who I rename Joseph K), who is possibly the most tedious person I have ever met and who must have her over for a meal to explain why a particular brand of quality solder is the most efficient conductor and you mightn't think it would make much difference but in the longer term it's best to be prepared for a wider range of applications for any instrument you might build. (Dida insists to him on the telephone before their meeting that I go everywhere with her and that she will be so happy if he would extend his already too-kind invitation to me, as she's sure we'll get on like the oldest friends in the world. She tells me that he is 'a sweet guy'. As sweet as root canal work, believe me.) Fifth, she decides to make two of whatever the thing is she's building, in case one fails. Sixth, in testing the compatibility of her instrument with my portable cassette recorder, she ruins my recording head. ('It works too damn well,' she explains.) Seventh, and finally, she is ready to go receive whatever Steve sends into the ether. 'But,' she says, 'we'll have to return to that dump of a winebar.'

Here, for the first time since we began our quest for the missing man, for the first time since my bad behaviour caused [Newspaper] to lose its position as best-selling serious reporting instrument for the city of New York, in this crummy little booze-kennel, Dida, Muffy and I act suspiciously. Believe me, we start by acting real natural, Muffy quiet and contained between the table legs, Dida and I wearing headphones as if sharing a special song, tapping out-of-time on the round faux-wood laminate of the tabletop. But we're listening to nothing. We watch Steve arrive and enter the hovel he probably calls an office. We listen to our headphones. Nothing. Dida follows the headphone wires down into the old airline bag that for years has made me look like a tourist in my semi-adopted city. She unplugs the wires from one of her devices and into the back-up. Zero reception. She fiddles with the dials. Zilcho. She replugs device one in and fiddles with its dials. Fuck all. She attaches an aerial wire to device one and holds it in the air with her left hand while she adjusts the frequency or amplitude or whatever the dial is supposed to do with her right. This produces some response: something momentarily clicks in my ears.

'Hold this!' she orders, handing me the aerial wire. She uncoils more wire from the airline bag, until about six or eight yards of wire are spaghettied on the table.

'Your 'phones, take them off.'

I do.

'Now, take the end of the wire towards the door, hold it as high as you can . . . Great. Keep going. All right. Hold it there for a second.'

The barman and the two drinkers at the bar follow my progress across the floor, one of the drinkers actually open-mouthed.

'This is really good, Vern. Try and hook it above the door there.' I drag a barstool towards me with my foot. When it arrives, I stand on it and begin to attach the wire to the doorframe.

'Vern? It's best if you just stay right there. This is really great reception. It's clear as a bell.'

I balance there for what must be half an hour. Three or four customers arrive, stare at me briefly, then watch a TV up the other end of the bar. As they say in America, thank God for baseball. Yes, it sure gives the circuses a rest. I try to look professional, like I'm adjusting or measuring or installing. This is what I'm doing in my mind. I see the barman look up at me from time to time and shake his head. No doubt he's seen more ridiculous activities in here later at night, but I don't want to know. Dida is paying little attention to my predicament or to me. She's listening to her headphones, lips tightened, nodding now and then, making minor dial twiddles. Then she gives me a nod and says, 'That's it.' We leave, and no one has noticed a thing we've done.

As we make our way back to the apartment, I feel an overwhelming sense of accomplishment. This information we have gathered—much as ancient humans gathered berries from thorny bushes and certain roots and fungi from between hard rocks and difficult to access crevices—I sense this information will be delectable. We've gathered the luxury item and, having done so, we now possess a luxury margin: there is no hurry. The cat is in the bag, the conspiratorial bird is in hand, and the little white dog is more or less at heel. We will savour the anticipation of decoding by fulfilling human sexual desires: desires which transcend the ages, which transcend whatever marginalia one gathers to supplement the wild rice and potatoes of contemporary information.

Back home, Dida and I recapture the quenching and satiation of our first weeks together. The logic which has made possible our cultural journey from winebar to bedroom is made up of philosophical leaps and bounds. It is a logic for mutual convenience and we admit it as we entangle.

'This,' cries Dida, 'is extremely advantageous.'

'Mm,' I reply, and repeat that syllable several more times for emphasis.

Codebreaking is boring. Don't believe the war movies. Even if the solution comes to the codebreaker in a momentary flash of genius, the weeks of application which follow are about as fun as copying out the US Constitution for class punishment. Australia, too, has a written constitution. I could set out to list all the nations of the world with written constitutions, then sort my list in Cyrillic alphabetical order, by area, size of population, principal exports, number of insects per head of population, percentage of dogs who are small, white and smart, and by dozens of other permutative classifications, and this exercise would be more interesting than copying down the coded transcript of fourteen minutes of tape, and rewriting it in decoded, accessible English.

I could complain all day and even that would be more exciting than a codebreaker's lifetime of highlights but I ought to admit that I undertake none of the transcription or translation of Dida's tapes. She does the lot, spending a headphoned day making page after page of dots and dashes, then two more days typing it up. The broadcast is pure Morse: hardly even rates as a code. Occasionally she calls out, 'Asterisk.' She theorises that the asterisks are interspersed between self-contained messages. If this is correct, the broadcast comprises a series of discrete messages. I contribute nothing to the process except for occasional comments like those in the preceding paragraph.

The decoded words themselves I can almost immediately place—'Space Alien Baby "Found in Cocoa Krispies": US Colonel' and 'Japanese Soldiers on Moon' were two of the more outlandish. They were from [Newspaper]'s supposedly whacky 'Zany Page', a weekly feature conceived by the editors to gain market share among tabloid readers. I'd been the named editor for the five weeks Zany Page survived. By the fourth week I had nothing new to include, the journalists having run out of imagination, so I re-ran the stories from the first week. But that wasn't the reason for axing the page—the same stories show up on the news pages again and again, without complaint from readers: 'Wine Drinkers Live Longer'; 'How the I.R.S. Cheats

Us'; 'Aren't Famous People Amazing?' Zany Page was axed because advertisers didn't like it. They couldn't tell whether it was good or bad; good short-term and bad long-term; or good numbers and bad profile; or bad numbers and good youth potential; or important product repositioning and tremendous loss-of-face. Following the alien baby story, a rival breakfast cereal advertiser complained. That was pretty much the end of Zany Page. The memories of newspaper life . . . they churn and churn.

After fourteen decoded minutes, I figure out that I'd edited every story included in Steve's broadcast. Every single one. No exceptions.

What? I did what? Was I trying to do it? Was I in on this plot, whatever it was? I don't remember conspiring to broadcast ridiculous newspaper space-fillers. I don't remember conspiring to do anything. I couldn't, as the saying goes, conspire my way out of a wet paper bag. All my little fibs and appropriations have been totally solo. Plotting would be completely out of character. What's more, I'm a dedicated print-media man and wouldn't touch that broadcast stuff with a greased barge pole.

So, what's happened to me? What has been done? I try to recall signs of tampering: new scar tissue above my hairline, unusual yearnings or brain-pain. On any occasion in the past, have I lost an hour or a day? Recently, has my behaviour appeared unusual or out of character? Well, yes, but that's L-O-V-E, not cerebral implantation, surely. How well do I know Dida? Was the point of tongue circling my ear and then darting to its centre actually pressing a miniature transistor into place? What about Muffy? When I got him, I believed he was a puppy, but I had no way of checking. He could have been a brilliant dwarf dog with a mind the size of

Saturn. On the other hand, the little doggie had tracked down the broadcast room. And furthermore, if Dida was on the other side, why has she just betrayed her employers by breaking the code?

Yep, Vern, hang on a single minute there. How could I suspect my most loved and loving companions? How could I doubt them and their motives while ignoring the (most probably) evil intentions of [Newspaper]? I ought to be ashamed. I ought to dig deeper into what [Newspaper] is up to. I ought to approach this in a reasoned and orderly manner, just as though I were obeying the instructions of airline personnel to assume crash-ready positions as we are about to make an unscheduled landing twelve thousand miles from the nearest airport. Something is going on in my head and I need to find out what it is. It is time to see a hypnotist. Muffy, I am sure, would agree.

Muffy: *Beneath the buildings and their concrete foundations, under the steaming asphalt, below railway lines and runways, the soil might remain viable. Perhaps it is lying fallow, waiting for some Styxian grain-farmer to scatter subterranean wheat, or for the tiny pockets of rich loam around indoor cacti to abandon their human-imposed limitations and join together like so many disparate yet coalescing slicks of oil, and to trickle through to the hidden soil, which, feeling a barely registrable pulse of oxygen, will break through the urban crust and sprout jungles of weeds, bringing disorder, chaos and apocalypse. Humans had better keep an eye on their houseplants.*

CHAPTER 5

I spend a few days in the City Library reading accounts by people who have survived hypnotherapy and memory improvement treatments. *I stayed young through self-hypnosis. I discovered my psychic potential. Hypnotism made simple, for beginners, for dinner parties, for office romance. Recover only the memories you want to recover, the ones that make you feel good, bad, rich, slightly taller, Ancient Egyptian, at all.* The library is too cold to spend many days in. The books are not dusty enough. Too many people have read these books when they should have been reading *One Day in the Life of Ivan Denisovitch* and Shakespeare's sonnets. Too many people have put themselves under instead of opening their minds to the world of surfaces and serfdom, arts and artifice. I think, I am about to join them.

Dida has a close friend who will help me in this. Dida assures me her friend is well known in the hypnotism field and is a nice woman too. She understands that people may not feel all that comfortable with exposing their internal workings and she's sensitive to that. Dida would trust her. She's helped other friends of Dida's. Dida just wants to make it easier for me. If I find it a problem that Dida's friend knows Dida personally, Dida is sure her friend would refer me on to someone else of equal hypnotic talent. Our path towards the mystery's solution is clear and simple.

MUFFFFYYYYYYYYYY!!!!!!!! HELP! Reading all these books and book covers, the only discovery I make about myself is this: I do not want to be hypnotised. I am a self-control freak. But I decide to go ahead. I can think of no other solution.

The next three days, Muffy and I do a lot of walking. We don't talk very much, but when we stop for a rest on our walks, Muffy sits on my knees and licks my face.

Muffy: *Some weeks are full of journeys, every day a new trajectory. The hours carry the spirit of the enterprising traveller. The man bears an ambulatory ambience in each whistle, gesture, impulse. The man goes out and forgets human purpose. He strides out and then collapses, forgetting food, forgetting play, forgetting everything but the contact of skin with fur. The man goes out into the city but not through it. He behaves unlike his previous behaviour and unlike the behaviour of most other humans. The man makes a noise which means me, and we go out and he then neglects to maintain intention. He says the me-word and I go to him and he makes contact with my underfur and I tongue at his protuberances. He says the me-word a few times, but I cannot respond more as I am already fully responded. The man is not himself.*

What is going on with these people? I know that [Newspaper] is anxious to regain my editing skills. Although my departure has meant a drop in circulation of only a few per cent, the newspaper has fallen back a place against rival publications. Two per cent fewer readers can have disastrous repercussions for advertising sales. Revenue has probably dropped significantly already. The price of [Newspaper] shares continues to slip. I am certain [Newspaper]'s management would try plenty, including threats, to convince me to return. But is my return to [Newspaper] the purpose of the threats of litigation and the actuality of the kidnapping?

It does not come close to explaining why Steve is broadcasting my stories to strangers. It's not as though I've ever written or rewritten anything enlightening. No one wears badges with my picture or talks about the gurufication of Vernon. I'm not even a registered trademark. Nonetheless, someone wants something from inside my head. Someone must have done something inside my head to make me, Vernon Collins, desirable. Perhaps someone has caused me to utilise my skills in foreseeable and manageable ways. Maybe [Newspaper] or EIC or Steve has been foreseeing and managing my skills for its or EIC's or Steve's benefit. I thought love and Dida had brought me freedom, but the men from [Newspaper] want me back in post-hypnotic chains.

I came close to returning to my job. Terrifyingly close. Only Dida's intervention saved me. How easy it would have been to ask for my old desk back, my old terminal, the copy coming in same as before, my job perfectly delineated, my duties clear, my obligations strictly limited, my pay predictable and in the middle of the eighth decile, me still a young enough man, with good prospects. And they could have kept on fucking with my brain, if that's what they were doing, which seems very likely, whoever the hell 'they' are.

And now some other person, a friend of Dida's,

someone who's only human, after all, wants to go in there, to invite me to leave my own intracerebral room; she's going to go in to my brainbox and have secret conversations with parts of my mind inaccessible even to me. I've no choice but to let her, except to let someone most likely even weirder do it, *some friend of a hypnotist who is also a hypnotist*, someone who may know no one but other hypnotists. No way. The real choice is to go to Dida's friend or leave the implant in there, if there is one, assuming this woman can find it, if it's there. I decide—or, as it seems, the decision is thrust upon me—that, much in the manner of post-trauma antivenene, a second mindfuck is the only treatment for an earlier one.

OK, Dida, I'll go through with it. Dida gives me a scrap of paper bearing the name Jane Streeton and a phone number. I make an appointment with Dida's friend for the following day at 11 a.m.

The hypnotist's name is Jane Streeton, and her office is on Jane Street. Great. A victim of personalised-numberplate syndrome. Did she purposefully lease a room there or was it the only suitable room on the entire island? Was the room the only one available of that quality and suitability? Did she consider some slightly worse rooms and wish there was an equally good room so she wouldn't have the name thing; or were there rooms only very slightly better, so she took the name thing into account, giving it a certain but not overwhelming weight in coming to the decision to lease this room? Did she petition the City of New York to change the name from Stuyvesant Street South to Jane Street, with the Commissioner for Names and Renaming—her father—very happy to comply? Did she change her own name from Alfonsetta Eugenides to match the address? Did she believe the name Jane

Streeton was a past-life name, the memory triggered by her move to the room I will visit? What kind of a car does she drive, anyway, and what is its number-plate?

At 10.59 a.m. I knock on the door. The hypnotist opens it and waves me in to the room. Jane Streeton's office has two certificates on the wall and two four-drawer filing cabinets in a corner. I glance across the surface of the desk, looking for watchchains or whirling spirals or other hypnotic paraphernalia. I see none.

Apart from 'hello', the first words Jane speaks to me are, 'I guess you're not looking forward to this too much.'

Maybe she's going to hypnotise me by saying dozens of incredibly obvious things in a row. I tilt my head in response, meaning: well, no, but I'm not going to answer stupid questions anyway. She nods slowly a few times, nodding her whole torso without moving her neck. So much for small-talk and relaxation. Business.

'What do you want to discover here?' She manages not to sound combative. I explain that I think someone may have been tampering with my brain, that I think I am being used by bad people as some sort of medium, and that I believe I may be unwittingly conveying such messages through my editing work.

'Ah,' she replies. Halfway through recounting my problem to her, I begin to see its flaws. I suspect she too believes my logic to be outside that generally described as 'rational'.

'We'll see what we can do,' she says. I am relieved not to see her reach under her desk for the emergency button, and also pleased that four orderlies do not burst through her door and restrain me.

'Thank you,' I say, for something other than she probably imagines.

The results of the hypnosis: I still feel terribly guilty about a relationship I had in my late teens. I should never have implied all that deep love stuff and I'm really sorry we didn't get to talk much after the break-up. I hope you're very happy now, though I doubt it, considering that immediately after our split you got together with a guy I know is nowhere near your equal intellectually or in personality. I seem to believe I am to blame for you having married this guy. I don't know if you ever think of me any more, but if you do, I really wish you could forgive me. Maybe I'll call you next time I'm in Adelaide, Australia. Look, the first few times were really fun and I really did like going out with you for a while. I'm so sorry about what happened after that. I really am.

That's it? What about the conspiracy? Nothing? Nothing.

'Have you had similar feelings of persecution in the past?' Jane Streeton asks quietly.

'It's not a feeling,' I tell her. 'It's a thought.'

As for the possibility of an implant, on my pissed-off way home I buy a box of nails and catch a bus forty blocks uptown. I tuck a nail behind each ear. I walk through the security door at the entrance to the Mexican Consulate. The metal detector alarm beeps like crazy and the security guards say, 'Excuse me sir, would you please step behind this screen.'

They wave a hand-held metal detector over my body. It squeals when they bring it to my head.

I say, 'Oh, how embarrassing. I've got nails tucked behind my ears.'

I remove the nails, and they continue to check my scalp and mouth with the detector. Like the hypnotist, the metal detector pronounces my head to be interference-free, once the nails have gone. Nonetheless, the security guards refuse me admittance.

'You don't really want to go to Mexico, do you?' one asks, his intonation giving the reason: 'Because you have no idea who or where you are'.

'Mexico?' I retort. 'Is this not Hardware World?'

'No, my friend. It is not. Please go outside and see if what you want is there.'

I leave, mission accomplished. When I arrive home, I announce to Dida, 'My head has the all-clear.'

'I'm very pleased.' she says. 'I've always believed the problem wasn't particularly your brain. Isn't Jane nice?'

'Sure,' I say. 'If you like people who ask you about girlfriends it's taken you fifteen years to forget.'

'I think I'm about to become one of that sort of person, too,' says Dida. 'Tell me . . .'

Dida believes in a hierarchy of logics. She fully supports rational explanations when magical explanations can provide no advantage. She believes randomness is more likely than supernature. She has confessed that she wrote to [Newspaper] complaining that my Zany Page promoted ignorance and superstition. She thinks it is an amazing coincidence that we met, that I was walking Muffy past where she was fixing mobile phones that day in the park. We found each other, she believes: we were not *meant* for each other. Coincidence, and not fate. And, she decides, taking a further logical step away from primitive belief systems, there must be reasons linking my stories, Steve disappearance and regained sight, the appearance of the hat in the forest and the broadcasts. Coincidence is not enough. As for me, I'm way ahead. I've scaled Mount Reason and have come halfway down the other side.

'Yes! Yes!' I shout. 'Conspiracy!'

'No,' she rebukes. 'I want motives. An orderly problem requires an orderly response.'

Meantime, as if we don't have enough trouble coming at us from outside, this letter is pushed under the door.

September 16, 199___

Caretaker, Apt 212

Mr E. Smyth
Apt 723

Dear Mr Smyth,

It has been brought to the attention of the Strata Authority (incorporating the Body Corporate) that you may be keeping a dog or similar animal in your apartment.

You will note that Strata Regulation 6 specifically forbids all four-legged animals being kept in apartments.

If in fact you do have a dog or similar on the premises, you may be forced to move (or, if a tenant, evicted) and/or you may be subject to considerable fines administered both by the Strata Authority (empowered under Articles of Association 21(d)) and the City Health Department.

You have seven (7) days to respond to this letter. If a satisfactory response is not received by me at apt 212 within that time, action will be taken to evict you and said animal from the premises.

Yours faithfully,
H.I. Grenfield,
Caretaker

'Who the fuck is E. Smyth?' ask Dida, reading over my shoulder.

'He is that part of me who is a tenant,' I explain. 'Eddie Smyth is my lessee self.'

Dida ignores the humour.

'Your lease is in a false name?'

'Can't be too careful.'

My response to the letter is defence, defence, defence. What with the court case approaching and the very real chance of fines or good behaviour bonds, I don't need any further blemishes on my personal profile.

Dear Mr Grenfield,

I am sorry and a little embarrassed about the disturbances which may have caused my neighbours to believe I was keeping a dog (or, very occasionally, a herd of elephants!). Most weekends my young nephew stays with me (note that my apartment is licensed for up to two (2) occupants). Unfortunately, his current favourite CD is '101 Dalmatians', which he insists on 'barking' along to. I shall endeavour to keep him a little quieter in future, but apologise for any minor inconvenience his youthful enthusiasm and mediocre musical taste may have caused my neighbours.

Contritely,
Edmund (Eddie) Smyth
Apt 723

I strongly suspect the eviction threat was instigated by the same people who have been harassing me ever since [Newspaper] began to lose profitability—no doubt the caretaker received the dog information in a note signed 'a friend'. Following this latest blow, I become more careful walking Muffy. I transform my old airline bag into a doggie carry-case with plentiful yet hidden airholes, and teach Muffy to become excited at the prospect of his confinement therein. This doesn't take very long: Muffy is a very excitable dog-ness. I then teach him to restrain his expressions of excitement to wagging and salivating rather than whining and barking. He is extremely receptive to the training, which is backed up by such sanctions as the pointing finger and the cross look, or rewarded with the biscuit. Dida is similarly stern and generous with him.

Muffy learns so much in a week, but Dida and I have learnt nothing.

Muffy: *When one human approaches another, there are always different sounds but similar emphases. The dog cannot predict how two members of the populace will behave towards one another. They already know the appropriate responses when they meet, as if such responses were predetermined. The dog, though, has not the foresight to predict the manner in which the two humans will respond to one another and can only observe the interactions as they occur. The members of the populace do not sniff at each other nor, generally, do they wrestle one another to the ground. Nonetheless, the human, like the dog, wants some-thing. Can the approached human prolong the approacher's life? The knots of veins or arteries across muscle surfaces are fragile reminders of mortality.*

In winter, points of air fall from above and fracture the ground. Now, presumably, the points are winding their ways skyward. I am swinging back and forth in the dark. Here is a point of air. And—look!—here is another. Outside, the points come together. In the big air, humans and dogs approach and recede.

Regarding the broadcasts, the time has come for some basic document research. For an old newspaper-man such as I am, research means looking through old newspapers. Dida and I take daily, dog-free journeys to the City Library to scan the stories named in Steve's broadcast and any other stories I'd worked on that may or may not have been named in previous broadcasts. We leave Muffy with Phil, my neighbour, who has not yet moved to Maryland but sees Julia every day because she has moved in with him. I like to think that Muffy contributed to the development of Phil and Julia's parental feelings.

Dida takes Phil a copy of the 'Japanese Soldiers' story and asks him what he thinks. I go along with her.

'This some lateral-thinking problem?' he asks me.

I give a non-committal nod. He looks all around the story, holds it up to the light, turns it over.

'No hidden pictures?'

'I don't think so,' I say. 'Not of that sort.'

'And it's from [Newspaper]?'

'Yes.'

'Oh, I see what you're getting at. You wrote this, did you Vern?' He reads a couple of paragraphs. 'I'm impressed.'

'Rewrote it, really.'

'I think it's very good, for what it is. After all, it's not meant to be Whitman, is it?'

'Phil,' says Dida, 'that's not the answer we're after. We want to know what else could be significant about this story.'

'Hmmm. I guess that it's total fiction isn't relevant?'

'Right.'

'The by-line. H. Ackpen. That's it. That's the joke?'

'No,' says Dida.

I add helpfully, 'The nom de plume is how contemporary journalists take responsibility for their words.'

'It's the regular typeface?'

'It is.'

'More lateral, huh?'

'Yes.' Dida is doing the light-hearted school teacher: brusque, but smiling.

'I don't know what she's getting at either,' I comfort him.

'Oh, I know. It's the date, isn't it? It's got to be. September 20, huh? That was the day before gold broke four hundred and fifty dollars,' he says. 'Very historic.'

Dida kisses him. 'That's exactly it,' she tells him. 'You're the first to guess.'

I shake my head. I thought I was nuts, but Dida is out of her head.

'Thanks, Phil.' My eyes tell him: 'Nothing to do with me.'

'Gold? I have nothing to do with gold,' I protest once we're back in our place.

'Of course you do. They must want your stories for something, and they must want you for much the same reason. Rule out jealousy: they already have more material possessions than you, and more access to intelligence—even if you'd win hands down one-on-one any day. Rule out love: there's no attempt to win me over. Rule out information: Jane, a professional seeker of information, has found your mind empty. What's left? Money. So, we check these stories against any money moving around at much the same time.'

'Come on,' I say. 'Come off it.'

'You have a better theory?'

I don't, but . . . 'That's so far-fetched. How did you come up with an idea like that?'

'You keep mentioning conspiracies. Nothing could be more conspiratorial than a cartel manipulating share and commodity prices.'

'But,' (I am running out of objections here) 'why would Phil know that stuff?'

'Doesn't he talk to you about his investments?'

'We talk about cars and baseball.'

'There you go.'

I find it hard to believe I could be at the centre of a vast money making, laundering or moving network and not know anything about it. Neither does Dida's explanation help me understand why my former job, my person, and a bunch of large and nasty men should converge. Serious journalists ask who, what, when, where and why. I'm left with Zany Page journalism, the one question raised by brilliant stories such as 'Human Lightning Rod Unwelcome in Fort Worth'— 'Why me?'

I am sceptical of Dida's explanation, but for the sake of the exercise, I do my part. We note all items substantially rewritten by me in the six-month period prior to my departure from [Newspaper], and graph them against currency fluctuations, stock-market and futures movements, building applications and approvals, company registrations, and net holdings of major banking corporations. Each day, according to Dida, I have contributed something. Sometimes the market moves up, sometimes it moves down and sometimes it is steady. So far, no good. We have the theory, but it applies to everything or to nothing or to some things we cannot identify.

We try to devise some kind of content measure. Story quality against market response. But what is quality? My writing or rewriting has no quality. It's journalism. Story themes? Repetitions of myths?

Vocabulary? Some kind of signal in the headlines? We plot subject matter, headline, length of article and size of accompanying photographs or illustrations (if any) against movements of various relevant indicators. More dead-ends.

I return to my computer and to *: *Urban Interstices*. It is easier to edit this time because I am convinced it has no meaning. I could treat it as journalism, but I decide to add elegance rather than simplicity. I treat it as advertising. By the end of the day I have completed several articles: slick, bland and full of in-house, insubstantial style. I do not know whether the magazine will ever show up in print, but its potential matches every other magazine I can think of.

I finish the job late the next afternoon and ring Sarah Kadaré at the agency. She has been meaning to call me and arrange to meet for a friendly, introductory drink but she's been totally snowed under, not to mention stretched, flat chat, flat out and in vital meetings with clients whose names she will not mention regarding their imminent receptions of vast sums for virtually no work. One day I too will receive fees for associating my name with well-regarded publications. Still, that's some way off unless I commit major crime—ha ha—and it's important in the meantime to establish a reputation for honest, workmanlike jobs and she looks forward to receiving the edited magazine and is sure its newfound solidity will be tangible. I press SEND, and the replicated magazine instantaneously appears at the agency. The cheque will follow within fourteen days because she prides herself on speedy reward for speedy work. Click.

I stare out the apartment window, recovering from the conversation. I had contributed only the words, 'I've finished the magazine job.'

Across to the southeast a new skyscraper is reaching completion. I realise it is the first time I have seen it: fifty storeys high and of the blue, reflective glass which could place it in any city in the world. Sydney, Philadelphia, Singapore. Below, with the dusk, street-lights flick on. At the summit of the building, a sign illuminates: *. Someone is making a lot of money.

So, with the rent covered for a few weeks, once my cheque arrives from the bogus employers, there is nothing to do except play detectives some more. I've seen children playing 'offices' with more authority than I feel photocopying and sorting articles which preceded sudden, unexplained rises in various stocks. Children become possessed by their roles. I have no such confidence. If anything possesses me, it is futility. Another pointless filing exercise. I group stories pre-ceding rises in metals or construction and stories preceding jumps in the dollar or drops in the yen and deutschmark. Here they are, low piles of A4 copy paper. I transform the City Library's yellowing curls of newspaper and print-outs from its CD-ROM archive—every item out of date and now something other than news—into evenly sized piles of clippings. Now they follow other, externally imposed storylines whose outcomes and morals have yet to be deter-mined. Perhaps they will turn out to be about the pervasiveness of corporate crime, or perhaps about greed before a fall. My role is not yet properly defined either. I can't be sure whether I'm a player or a piece.

Here the stories are, all piled next to my computer. I could begin to log them on to the computer. I don't. At some deep level of my mind, the sort of district Jane Streeton would have been happy promenading up and down, the clipped stories begin to look soft, inviting and rather pillow-like. I fall asleep.

This is the dream I have: a man is walking ahead of me along a long straight road in rural Australia. The grass to either side of the road is yellow, or sunburnt white. The surface of the road is clay-orange. The man walks ahead and I follow, running, trying to catch up to him. The wind blows in my face. I cannot narrow the distance between us at all. I try to call out, but can only make a wordless, donkey-like braying noise which the man can't hear. I am breathing hard, panting with the effort of running while all he does is walk. This seems to last a very long time. At last I begin to get closer to him, until I am only twenty or so yards behind. Then I realise the man is on the other side of a ravine and that there is no means of crossing. I try once more to call out. This time he turns around. I see the man has no irises. He smiles mockingly. I think: he can see me.

I wake perspiring. A clipping has stuck to my forehead and I peel it off. I go to the bathroom to wash my face. As I look in the mirror, I see a mark where the clipping had been. The mark is the page number B26. Tick tick tick bzzzzzzztbing! That's it! Page numbers! 'Dida!'

The serious-boring business of logging page numbers against price movements takes me several days. It should have taken about half a day, but data entry is not a task I warm to. Consequently, I find many more pressing demands on my time: dusting around cupboards, cleaning the oven, testing new varieties of dogfood with Muffy, who does like chicken every day after all.

By the end (of the data entry, not the dogfood), something is taking shape. Dida points out that Section A appears to correspond with industrial stocks and Section B with metal prices, while C and D tend to predict movements in mining stocks and the futures market, respectively. Still, she notes, these are only tendencies. We have a practicable hypothesis, OK, and one against which we can measure and test results. The problem is that there are many more exceptions to it than examples of it in operation.

Next, we must distinguish the operational stories from the exceptions. Length and position on the page do not relate to size of movement. Type-size of headlines? No. Pseudonym of journalist? No.

Later that week, as we are sitting in the bath comparing pubic hair thicknesses, Dida works it out.

'How does that Japanese soldiers story begin?' she asks.

' "About the last thing anyone would expect to find on the moon is a Japanese soldier",' I quote, pretty impressed with myself for such an amazing memory feat. She acknowledges with a cursory nod; she had remembered it too.

'And the "Space Alien Baby"?'

' "About seven o'clock this morning, nine-year-old Virgina Hudson . . .".'

'Yes! What about "Second-Chance Swim Champ Triumphs at Last"?'

' "About halfway through his history-making four-hundred-metres butterfly comeback race . . .",' I recite. I'm thinking, Something is similar in all of the above, but what the fuck is it?

'Yes!' shouts Dida, slapping her palms on the water surface. 'All the effective stories begin with "About"!'

I slap the water, too, shouting, 'Of course! You're a genius!'

Dida dives forward and I slide back till only my nose and knees are above the surface, our tongues swirl with the eddies of bathwater, and we celebrate Dida's genius in the customary manner.

That evening I reflect on my former career. Had I fallen into lazy and formulaic journalistic practices?

Don't, Vernon A admonishes me, don't be oxymoronic. 'Journalistic practices' already implies laziness and formulism.

Oh come now, says Vernon B. What happened to our bright-eyed Australian boy? What happened to journalism with depth and intelligence?

He developed, says A. He didn't 'fall' into anything. He became reliable.

Too reliable, it appears, replies B.

No such thing. Copy is copy. Our man filled out the space between the car ads better than anyone else in the business. He was so predictable, readers' eyes would slide from his stories, across the page, and fix on those all-important logos, those trademarks the US government fights all around the world to enforce. Our Vernon no doubt played a positive role in strengthening whatever they call the ANZUS alliance nowadays by selling these new cars. A strong USA means a strong Australia.

Fat lot of good it's done us, argues B. He tries to give up his job—for perfectly adequate reasons—and discovers this is not an option. He doesn't realise how effective he has been. He probably isn't even conscious that the forces of capital have befuddled his formerly clear and concise style to the point where he has become useful.

You are too confused, says A in what is supposed to be the clincher. He addled himself. It's called career path.

We cannot be sure they were his genuine words and

not some implant. Who knows whether, given other circumstances, he would have chosen to write in that manner? B comes back with.

Beginning a large number of stories with 'About' sounds very much like personal style to me, parries A.

A word does not a style make, especially if it is immediately parasitised by rich strangers for as-yet-unknown purposes probably connected with large amounts of money, B insists.

Therefore, concludes A in a burst of existential self-congratulation, our man is indispensable. What a position to be in. And, I might add, a position changed not one whit since we conceived of Vernon as a being acting in the world.

Thinking too much on the question 'Am I still me?' gives me a new characteristic: a migraine. Formerly, I had been secure in barracking on the 'nurture' side of the nature/nurture divide.

'Definitely a liberal,' colleagues told me when I denigrated yet another column on the natural strength and analytical prowess of American men. 'With that attitude, you'll never make the transition to management.'

But recent events seem to have redefined nurture as 'sudden and secretive brain-tampering'. Somebody's nurturing of me has resulted in useful though unconscious behavioural patterns. That there is no detectable sign of tampering proves nothing to my intuition on the matter. Somehow I have been taught to channel financial predictors to unknown investors. This revelation does not help my ego, no matter how vital I have become in the role of 'tool'. So much for liberalism.

Perhaps I've always been a repressed (U.S.) Repub-

lican or (Australian) National Party supporter. I consider switching loyalties, but the nature alternative is
no better. If I am a genetically determined man rather
than a result of environmental forces, what kind of a
newspaperman am I? My natural state is exposed as
that of a dully conventional or conventionally dull
sub-editorial practitioner with approximately three
turns of phrase.

Having reasoned myself through to this point, I am
not terribly happy. On the one hand, I am determined
not to be determined. On the other, I want a free will
which is capable of something beyond the world's
most predictable journalism. For the moment, I reach
automatistically for the medicine cupboard. Head
aches, fix headache, some force beyond my tiny self
insists. I hope my namebrand extra-strength headache
pill will assist me in achieving at least that small aim.
It does. It eases the pain and I sleep. I wake many,
many hours later when a small dog moistens my cheek
with his tongue.

Muffy: *A dog, at least, is consistent. He or she responds
to similar stimuli in similar ways, and for good reason. A
bone always makes a dog happy, the prospect of a walk and
some tree-sniffing always makes him or her excited, the
withdrawal of a promised snack is invariably unfortunate.
The chance to test out new streets in pursuit of person,
persons or vehicle/s known or unknown is irresistible.*

*But what is it with people? They forget how to behave
from one day to the next. They change their eating habits
and cannot remember to be diurnal. A dog does all she or
he can to maintain a steady relationship, but at times it
becomes extremely difficult to do that. Some people do not
always wish to be reminded 'I am a dog in your company'.
Why is that? The dog is consistently uncertain on this
matter. She or he continues to remind, and it is for the*

person to embrace or rebuff and for the dog to search for pattern.

To my mind, Americans are supposed to be highly skilled neurotics and Australians comfortable in any situation, no worries, yet Dida is perfectly at ease and I have practically gnawed my fingers off with anxiety. Am I too American already, more American than Americans? Are the old myths shot to pieces, like my nerves? Dida denies she is exceptional.

'I don't know,' she says. 'I simply do what it occurs to me to do. If a guy disappears and reappears as someone else, I become too curious to say, "Ah well, such is life in the big city." I want to find that guy. Most Americans would feel the same.'

'They would? What happened to "don't get involved"?'

'You don't want to find your friend or acquaintance or whatever you call him? Vern, I thought you felt the same as me: you don't appear too chicken. Anyway, from what I've seen in the movies, given a chance you Australians would form some kind of feral collective and go hunting for him with pruning hooks and sling-shots.'

'I'm surprised at you,' I tell her. 'I thought you knew me better than that.'

'Perhaps you just don't know any other Australians to collectivise with.'

I sulk for a while. I guess Dida's explanation of Australians is as likely as mine of her compatriots. Am I conditioned not by a pentothal cocktail but by nation-ality? Would Lincoln handle this mystery better than Chifley? Would I rather have Ned Kelly on my side or Billy the Kid? Would ASIO get to the bottom of all this before the CIA did? Would I send Skippy for help before I sent Mr Ed? If this happened in Australia, would I know what to do better than I do when it happens in New York City? Should I step outside, breathe deeply until I've absorbed New York into every corpuscle of my blood, eat New York hotdogs until every fat cell contains a part of this city, drink gallons of New York water until New York flows through me like the Hudson River moves through it; and if I undertake all this, will my entire body sense what to do next?

Dida has already decided.

'I think it's time to return to the paper for a few days,' she says. 'Rewrite one of your "About" stories and we'll try to predict market outcomes. We should write the predictions on a piece of paper and safeguard them, sealed and dated, in a safety deposit box. If we're right, we've got Evidence.'

'Well OK. I'm not exactly sure what the Evidence will be of, though.'

'It's bound to be Evidence of something. If we find the cartel, the discovery might come in handy for your court case.'

'Don't remind me,' I say. November 14 is too near. I guess if a sealed envelope can get me off those charges, it's a good idea. That's probably what a plea bargain is: the envelope or the box, with the latter as a large grey building with barred windows and grumpy waiters. I mutter about prison.

'I don't think you're going to prison, Vern,' Dida tries to reassure me. 'They're trying to scare you again. Maybe if you go back to work they'll drop the charges.'

Maybe. I doubt it.

I telephone Eisie who says, 'Vernon, that's fantastic. We're all looking forward to seeing you again, even those who have no idea you're coming back. See you tomorrow!'

'The charges, Eisie. Can you fix up that small matter?'

'Sure, mate,' he says in repulsive fake Australian. 'I'll have those suspended immediately.'

'Suspended? You mean "dropped".'

'Whatever.'

Back at work, the very first story to leave my terminal begins with 'About'. I post a print-out to myself. Eisie is very pleased to see me and stops by several times to tell me. He gloats slightly when he speaks, but at least he makes no reference to the kidnapping or to Steve. He says, 'We must do lunch later this week. Thursday, maybe, or Friday. I'll confirm that for you later.'

I grunt in reply. It is difficult to decide on a position to take in relation to him. The bastard kidnapped me. He tried to bully me back to the job and must now believe his bullying was successful. I have no reason to forgive him, yet if I am openly hostile to him he may suspect that I suspect something deeper than veiled threats and deprivation of liberty. On the other hand, if I'm actually friendly, he may think I have forgiven him. Eventually I choose 'wounded' as the correct approach. I'll take his criminality and violence towards me as a personal affront, a betrayal after all our years together. I'm hurt that he had three goons toss me into the back of a van, because that is no way to treat an old friend. Consequently, whenever he comes in to say how wonderful it is to have me back on board, the old team together again, I pout and go silent. Let him apologise if he dares. Let him acknowledge he has done the wrong thing by me. Or if, as seems most likely, he continues to pretend nothing happened, let him suffer a sulky colleague every day until I abandon him a second time.

The first day of my return has been, I tell Dida, very successful. Eisie must surely be feeling extremely guilty, and any market movement following tomorrow's publication will prove our 'About' theory.

'Well done,' she says, nodding briskly—commander of a force dropped behind enemy lines. 'Now we shall see.'

I arrive at work early the next morning and grab a copy of the paper. I flick through Section B: there it is, the news item straight from a press release on new video-conferencing technologies.

'About sixty-five senior executives forgot they were in 65 different cities this morning, thanks to a device weighing less than a mobile phone,' I'd written. The published story no longer begins with 'About'. I guess its use was a little forced in the context, but the alteration probably has nothing to do with elegance of expression. I'll try again, but had better leave it a day or two. Fuck it.

There is a letter in my pigeonhole with a familiar crest on the envelope.

Justice Department of the State of New York
Post Office Box 1111, Central Post Office,
New York City, NY

Notice of Suspension

Re: People v Vernon Collins

Mr Vernon Collins is advised that charges pending against him, to wit:
three counts of wrongful appropriation
one count of grand theft
have been temporarily suspended by the Justice

Department of the State of New York following
intercession by its informant/complainant.

Mr Vernon Collins is further advised that the
Justice Department of the State of New York
reserves the right to re-activate said charges
within six (6) years of the date of this notice.

Further information concerning pending or suspended charges is obtainable from Mr Nicholson
S. Grant Snr, 3rd Assistant Deputy Vice-Secretary
of the Justice Department, on 212 JUSTICE/fax
212 333 FINE.

Yours sincerely,
Nicholson S. Grant Senior (Mr)
3rd Assistant Deputy Vice-Secretary
Justice Department of the State of New York

Fuck it again. Eisie has stretched the truth. He needs
to be brought down, I think to myself. He needs things
to go wrong for him, but I'm far too professional to
allow errors to pass through my terminal, far too
canny for them to originate there.

I blend back into work with ease. There is nothing
to learn. Stories are sent through to me, appearing
unheralded in my terminal as though I'd never been
away. Eisie forgets about lunch that first week, but
when slightly improved sales figures come in for the
fortnight following my return, I find theatre tickets in
my pigeon hole courtesy of EIC and accompanied by
a signed compliments slip on which is written, 'Welcome Back'. No one is likely to admit directly that the
pick up in sales is due to me and it will take some
time before occasional readers become regular again,
but I am dragging the voice of the paper Pacificwards
and that is very, very good for business. In the highly
competitive New York newspaper market, advertisers

will soon look favourably upon [Newspaper] again. Remember, as EIC once announced to a group of middle-level editorial staff, a thick paper is a good paper.

Two days later I rewrite the lead of a New York City crime story for metropolitan news—Section D: 'About six or seven armed bandits burst into the Bank of New York's Park Avenue branch at noon yesterday, escaping with over $500 000.' My version is considerably worse than the journalist's original copy. The next day, though, my rewrite appears in Section D of the paper, and my sealed, postmarked envelope predicting a rise in mining stocks arrives under the apartment door.

That day, a mining stock that has been quiet for months suddenly jumps sharply on heavy turnover. Could this be Evidence?

'Well,' I say, 'I don't think we've proved anything yet, but we haven't disproved it either.'

'So the hypothesis stands,' concludes Dida.

'But why me?'

'Because you seem to be trying to help them. You cannot help it. You boost their sales, you unconsciously tell them which stocks to trade in. You should either ask them for a very large raise or resign again.'

I'm a total wonder. I'm the little Aussie guy who can show the big kids how to play. I battle through and never give up. I'm unpretentiously heroic. I'm completely reliable.

'I didn't resign the first time,' I remind her. 'I just stopped going because of how attractive you are.'

No doubt abandoning work had been and is the correct tactic. I file three more 'About' stories before I redeploy it.

'Done,' I announce.

Dida smiles irresistibly. I throw my arms around her and she throws hers around me. Our legs intertwine. Our lips engage. We fail to maintain our balance.

CHAPTER 6

It's not many days before my colleagues at [Newspaper] realise they have become ex-colleagues again. Good ol' Eisie must miss me so much. He's too broken up to write on his own account. The only letter I get is from my regular correspondent.

Justice Department of the State of New York
Post Office Box 1111, Central Post Office,
New York City, NY

Notice of Continuance

Re: People v Vernon Collins

Mr Vernon Collins is advised that charges pending against him, to wit:
three counts of wrongful appropriation
one count of grand theft
have been reinstated following representations from complainants.

Mr Vernon Collins is ordered to appear at Manhattan Central Court 182 Avenue of the

Americas in its criminal jurisdiction at
9.30 a.m./p.m. on 28 November 199_ to answer
these charges.

Mr Vernon Collins is further advised that he will
be advised in the event of any addition to the
charges or of further postponement of the hear-
ing. Should Mr Vernon Collins obtain an
Attorney prior to the hearing, he should advise
Mr Nicholson S. Grant Snr, 3rd Assistant Deputy
Vice-Secretary of the Justice Department, on 212
JUSTICE/fax 212 333 FINE.

Yours sincerely,
Nicholson S. Grant Senior (Mr)
3rd Assistant Deputy Vice-Secretary
Justice Department of the State of New York

Somehow, I am no longer surprised. Even though
my trial has been postponed by only two weeks—
despite all that sucking up to Eisie—I feel . . . pleased.
Satisfied. Flattered. [Newspaper] is interested in me
because (1) I'm unselfconsciously magic and (2) I produce profitable data. I don't know how I do it: I just
am. I'm learning to feel at ease with myself as an
enigmatic being with a non-rational side. I am accept-
ing that the existence of this side in no way detracts
from my value as a person or as a lover.

On this last matter, Dida has been extremely sup-
portive.

'Your poor, wounded psyche,' she coos.

'Yes. Poor, poor me,' I agree.

Muffy sits beside me on the grass in the park on the
day following my second decision to disentangle life
from employment. Muffy approves of his irrational
owner: his affection does not diminish even after I've

become this magical being with strange uncontrollable powers.

Muffy: *The grass tickles the dog's stomach. The tree is over there. There is a bird. The bird will not tickle the dog's stomach even if the dog rolls over. The bird is in the tree. The dog lies on the grass. The bird chirrups. The dog listens to the bird. The grass tickles the dog. If the bird were to land on the grass, the dog would chase the bird. If the grass were to tickle the bird . . . Aah, but birds seem not to be ticklish. The person behaves as the tree, with the exception that the bird will not be in the person.*

Neither has Dida altered herself to enable the continuation of her love for me. This can be seen by the steadiness of her relationship with Muffy over the same period. If one were to consider Muffy as the control personality and me as the noticeably changed one: had Dida fundamentally altered to accommodate my changes, she almost certainly also would have altered in relation to Muffy. That Dida and Muffy's relationship is unchanged and, at the same time, that Dida maintains a seemingly consistent relationship with the greatly changed me, indicates, in my view, great flexibility on Dida's part.

Our lovemaking has a certain regularity to it: it is routinely rich and varied, but I have discovered Dida's limits. I propose that we fuck in a manner suggested by the patterns of intensity of stories through the pages of [Newspaper]. Human interest pieces require different breathing patterns to Wall Street scandals, and a front-page financial stink clearly has other sexual implications to one reported only on the business pages. I'm thinking way ahead to a drugs-in-sport story when Dida refuses.

'The bedroom is no place for your private life,' she

says. 'Literature, that's a different matter. But don't go bringing your workplace into our bed.'

It remains possible that any deep personal changes within me are illusory, mere perceptions—though, as a high school teacher of mine back in Sydney once put it, perception is also something, is it not? Whatever has happened to me, whatever I or others have done to myself, whatever fundamental or superficial processes I have been subjected to, I continue to think of myself as the same person. 'I' is not a dilemma to be resolved or endlessly puzzled over here.

Instead, I continue to worry about a hat. The questions are unchanged despite everything that has occurred. What was this hat doing in a forest? Is this stain after all a bloodstain? Surely it is, but I cannot throw off a residue of doubt. The same questions circle and circle. What does a former blind man have to do with forests, newspapers, coded broadcasts and shakedowns? Who is this guy? Why are cross-media—print and radio—events relevant to him? How could someone so well organised forget his hat, especially if it were a valued gift from a generous acquaintance? Why has he left his bow tie in the park? Does he recall his sightless existence or, better, *how* does he recall that existence? When I remember the past, I conjure up scenes in my mind. I may close my eyes to do this. What does Steve remember? Does he open his eyes and close his ears to remember? To him, the past might be a night which would not end and then ended. Or he may not have known that day was possible, in which case sight, however obtained, might have been a shock. Or he may for decades have been living two lives, one sightless and one seeing, each perfectly contained within its own parameters and, to him, uncontradictory. He may be unaware of his double life,

Dr Steve Jekyll and Mr Steve Hyde: the former charming, behatted, blind; the latter cold, calculating and expert in redundant broadcast technology.

I am warming to Dida's biographical approach, so long as she handles the interviewing.

'OK,' I tell her, 'let's have a look at the Steve file.'

She drags out her notes: pages and pages of transcript from what must be dozens of interviews.

'All this? It will take me weeks,' I protest.

She peels off the top page and reads out the executive summary in the monotonous manner stereotypical of list-readers: 'Steve M~ born May 31, 1951, late child to older parents. Although blind, nonetheless happy and carefree child, much loved by parents, family and neighbours. Parents, Maurice and Elizabeth (Liza), felt themselves enlightened, treated Steve same as two much older sisters. Steve had household chores, pocket money. Educated at home by specialist tutor. Elder sister, Beatrice, dedicated much time to teaching him. Became confident and reasonably independent. When ten years old, children teased him, threw rocks—Steve's first indication of difference to other children. Bea terribly upset when Steve arrived home with gashed forehead, Steve stoic. According to Bea, Steve comforted her, not other way around. After that, Maurice and Liza explained blindness to Steve, reinforced that being a nice person is more important than sightedness, told him of famous blind people throughout history, that blindness often associated with perspicacity.

'According to Bea, "Steve's a gentle, sympathetic man." She recounted he heard cat mewling in distance, followed sound and climbed tree by touch to rescue cat. Bea: "Steve's that type of person."'

Dida had telephoned a few of Steve's friends, each

of whom spoke of Steve's great humanity, how he had never let his handicap intrude on his life, what a wonderful, gentle-yet-wicked sense of humour he had. One described taking Steve driving one weekend in an empty carpark. Steve had insisted on trying for almost an hour, persisting until he succeeded, until he had managed to change smoothly from first to second and then into third gear whilst following the friend's 'left, hard left, turn harder!' directions. At the end Steve, still completely relaxed, realised the friend was a nervous wreck and said, 'You seem a little uptight. Would you like a lift home?'

'After parents' death in late 1970s,' Dida concluded, 'worked as counsellor for blind teens, collected for charities on commission.'

None of Dida's informants mentioned business interests. No one spoke of Steve's interest in radio or codes. No one suggested that any of his friends were ruthless hoodlums.

'I think,' I tell Dida, 'it's time to revisit Steve's sister. Perhaps he has visited her and shown her the miracle of his regained sight.'

'Good idea,' nods Dida, the little twist in her voice reminding me that it was her idea in the first place.

'You organise it,' I say. 'You do the interview. Muffy and I have other duties, don't we, Muffy?'

I open the airline bag and Muffy jumps in. I zip it up. In the lift, I can feel his stubby little tail thwack, thwack, thwacking from one side of the bag to the other. I wave at the caretaker, who moves as if to engage me in conversation.

'Talk later,' I yell and leave the building. Round the corner, I open the bag and Muffy jumps out, barking. A passer-by shakes his head at the poor-trapped-puppy scene, and keeps walking.

'He likes it,' I call after the disapprover. 'He chose the bag himself.'

I wink at Muffy, who licks my face. Our walks are necessarily longer these days to compensate for the lost walking distance from the apartment to the front of the building.

Muffy: *The dog is long-lived. As the dog ages, she or he grows then softens, speeds up and strengthens, then slows and weakens. The bladder gains and loses control. The eyes eventually weep. As the dog alters, neither is the city still or fixed. The city reaches into the air and stretches over water, or the air swirls between and through buildings and water fills the streets. Some parts of the city change complexion with regularity and some portions change once and remain in the new condition. Parklands move east and west by the width of a dog biscuit, or are swept under the shiniest of facades wrapped around the tallest of skyscrapers. That the city changes so much in the course of a dog's life proves the great duration of the dog's life. If the city were to have remained unaltered, then the dog would have lived only for a short time.*

The dog has also seen small changes in the populace. The members of the populace develop new habits. They acquire different items of attire. Their allegiances move like ripples across the surface of the East River, shifting the water level by an inch, but beneath, substantially the same.

When Muffy and I return, Dida is telling the phone, 'Uh huh. Uh huh. OK. Yes, thank you. Very much appreciate it. Sure. Sure. I'll see you soon then. Bye-bye. Mm, bye.'

When she hangs up, she orders, 'Come on, we're going to Bea's now.'

' "We"?'

'Yes, "we",' says Dida. 'It's your meandering career

path that's got us into all this. Go listen to the answering machine.'

I press PLAY. A static-riddled voice with Eisie's intonation tells me: 'Mr Collins, according to the Bureau of Statistics' figures for October, absenteeism is once more on the rise in the US. Surveys attribute this—perhaps the greatest threat to national productivity—to a growing "pressure gap" between at-work and at-home situations. A spokesperson for one major employer said the solution lies not in improved workplace stress-management practices, but in actively increasing stress outside. We look forward to your imminent return.'

'Ah,' I reply to the machine, then, to Dida, 'OK, I'm with you,' and to Muffy, 'we'll be back very soon. Bye-bye.'

Muffy sags in disappointment.

Bea is less welcoming than on our initial visit, and less welcoming than I'd guessed from the tone of Dida's telephone conversation. This time there's no greeting. She simply says to me, 'What do you want?'

I've brought a print-out of * magazine's editorial page, complete with the Steve photo. Dida holds it towards the still-locked screen door.

'You said I could visit. We wanted to show you this photograph,' says Dida, soothingly. 'If you would please take a look at it.'

'I said *you* could visit,' she says to Dida. I don't say anything. Bea grimaces, but unlocks the door, takes the magazine, and waves us in.

'My God,' she says. 'It's uncanny. It looks so much like him and yet it's not him. The mouth seems a little different. Can it be possible? It must be the brother. My God.'

'Bea?' questions Dida, straight into her 'ma'am' tone. 'The brother?'

'I was told Steve had a twin who died at birth.'

'You're kidding,' I blurt.

'Our mother didn't like to talk about it.' Bea ignores me, continues to address Dida. 'I asked her once or twice, but she always changed the subject. I thought that with Stevie being born blind, the brother may have had more severe birth defects. But this man, apart from being sighted, is identical to my brother. He has to be the lost twin.'

'That explains a lot. Perhaps too much,' Dida tells her, somewhat insensitively. 'Thank you very much. We appreciate it. *I* appreciate it.'

We get up to leave, but Bea remains sitting, wheezing slightly.

'Are you OK?' Dida asks her, softly. 'Get her a glass of water, will you, Vern?'

When I return, Dida is talking quietly to Bea, holding her hand. Bea takes the water and sips at it.

'I'm so worried for Stevie. I'm so worried,' she says.

When we arrive back at the apartment, Muffy senses something is wrong. He trots quietly from Dida to me and across to Dida again as we sit in the loungeroom trying to think of a next step.

'He has to be the brother. I thought there was something weird about that guy's voice,' I say. 'I noticed it was mid-western, I honestly did. My God. Him showing up must mean Steve has become caught up in something to do with the brother. They're certainly not the same person.'

'Probably different,' nods Dida. 'But we should try to confirm it. In favour of the twins theory is that Steve couldn't possibly regain his sight. Against it is what

Bea said: the death of the brother many years before. Hospital records will be step one from here.'

'Do we know which hospital?'

'No. But I think I can find out without disturbing Bea again.'

On our first visit, Bea had given Dida the number of an old family friend, Virginia Emerson. Dida telephones her, and we call on her in her retirement village in Queens. A radio on the kitchen bench blasts tabloid opinions throughout the unit, but Mrs Emerson—as she insists we address her, despite my 'call me Vern, all my friends do' attempt at ingratiation—doesn't seem to notice it.

'I'd offer coffee, but I've just this moment run out,' she tells us, waving us towards the sofa. As soon as we've taken our place, she adopts classical interviewee manner: smiling, good posture, precise, full-sentence answers. She remembers Steve's birth and recalls sitting with Elizabeth at Santa Teresa de Avila Private Hospital in Alphabet City, in Manhattan's southeast.

'I must say I was surprised to find her in a Catholic hospital. She was from good Presbyterian stock. Not a regular churchgoer herself, mind. Liza had a difficult labour, lasted more than forty hours if I remember correctly. We didn't say much to each other. I simply sat there and smiled at her for comfort. She looked grey and exhausted.'

'You sat with her as she gave birth?' Dida asks.

'Don't be silly. Of course I didn't. This was two days after. I didn't yet know that the child had been born blind. I'm sure Liza knew, though.'

'It was just the one child?' asks Dida.

'Oh yes,' says Mrs Emerson, 'though she and her husband had two daughters already, as you may know. Lovely girls, too. And they've become very fine women. They drop in on me from time to time, and they bring beautiful little pastries. It's always nice to have generous visitors.'

Having reminded herself that Dida and I have neglected to bear gifts, Mrs Emerson cuts short our interview.

'I'm very busy at the moment,' she tells us. 'I'm going out this afternoon, so I'll have to ask you to leave right away.'

She is already standing up and herding us towards the door.

'I'm sorry,' she says, 'I don't have much time for people who barge in and ask lots of questions.'

Dida and I smile and say, 'Goodbye. Thank you.'

'Goodbye,' says Mrs Emerson, and shuts the door behind us.

At Santa Teresa de Avila, we convince the clerk that I am Steve.

'Please,' I tell him. 'My shrink has told me the emptiness in my life is most likely due to a missing twin.'

I try to look drawn and desperate. Dida takes on 'pleading spouse'. The clerk, whose name badge is called Ronald, asks for ID.

'To make things worse, my wallet was just stolen,' I tell him, patting my purportedly empty back pocket. 'But I can tell you my birthdate and my parents' names.'

'Well, I really shouldn't do this . . .' says Ronald. He is wagging his head at us slightly, indicating he knows our story is probably two bucketloads of donkey crap, but even if it is, his fundamental decency isn't affected by its veracity or lack thereof.

'Thank you, Ronald. This is important to me,' I say, as sincerely as possible.

Dida looks as if her life is about to become easier. Ronald punches a few keys on his computer terminal. A printer buzzes, and Ronald hands us a print-out.

'Thank you, Ronald. That's very good of you,' I say. Dida nods.

'The spacing on this is really weird,' Ronald apologises. 'I'll do you another copy.'

The first print-out shows a boy, 8lb 4 oz, then a space, with parents Maurice and Liza. There is no mention of a twin, alive or dead.

The second copy also has a gap between the child's weight and his parents' names.

'Could this have been tampered with?' Dida asks Ronald.

'Well if it has, I didn't say nothing.'

'I knew it,' I say. 'I knew I could feel something.'

We walk off with the two print-outs.

'Don't you leave them lying around here,' Ronald calls after us. 'You hear me?'

I wave the papers in the air in acknowledgement, but do not turn around. As we leave the hospital grounds, I find I have crumpled them in my fist from holding them too tightly.

'I don't feel good about telling that story to poor old Ronald,' I say to Dida.

'I know. Neither do I. But someone is harassing you, and Steve might not be OK. On balance, we're trying to do good,' Dida reassures me.

'I guess so,' I say, trying to be reassured.

'Do you think the records have been fucked around with?'

'I guess so,' I repeat.

This second man has no remaining birth record. He

exists only as legend. So far as the City of New York understands, he is not of woman born. His entire narrative being comprises a family story, a story of which his mother was ashamed, one she refused to acknowledge. Perhaps as he lived his distant life he sensed this maternal shame. Is this what causes criminality? He might have felt what I pretended to the clerk at the hospital: a sense of something missing. It might have been the discovery of his twin—the realisation that, after more than forty years of singularity, he was double—that upset him, that produced the ultra-conservative architectural ideology and the ire he vented on Dida and me. Or: in a city full of causes and coincidences, his appearance and the blind man's disappearance might belong in the coincidence category. Perhaps he still does not know of his twin.

Or: the story could be a sham, a cautionary tale told to Bea and her sister by their mother, a parental warning that abandonment had been possible, that the two girls were only retained at whim, that at any moment the mother might transform into Medea and consume them as she had consumed their disappeared brother. The gap in the birth record may mean nothing. Or: the meaning of the lost brother story might have been that the sisters were retained because of love, because their parents loved them for themselves, and, in feeling love for their children, did so by choice. If the maternal tale theory is correct, the two men are twins by appearance, but are unrelated. They ought not to exist in the same space, they ought never to have encountered one another, so similar are they. The brother is like a force from another dimension in a science fiction movie. The planet is at risk. Their chance appearance in the same city has thrown New York life out of balance.

Or: Bea has made up the twins story herself, feeling

malicious or preyed upon, or taking a personal dislike to one or both of us. Or: Bea is a hireling charged with forcing me back to [Newspaper]. Or she is the brains behind the whole racket.

It's all an elaborate plot and it's all aimed at me. Do all questors ultimately arrive at this conclusion, I wonder, that the quarry is like a Siren on a too-near shore? With effort, I dismiss any theories centred around Bea's collaboration with the forces arrayed against me. Then, having lain awake for the uncountable hours across the middle of the night, I fall asleep.

Dida and I have silently dismissed the chance-encounter-of-doppelgangers hypothesis and have, with equal silence, agreed to the rightness of one or other variation of the twins theory. As a result, we take to calling the sighted twin 'Steve', with quotemark gestures for emphasis, as against Steve, without. We seem also to have decided that 'Steve' is the impostor and Steve is the genuine article. Discussing two Steves causes some awkwardness in conversation, especially if we cannot look out for dit-dat gestures, as when one of us is watching TV or working. For example:

'I wonder what's happened to "Steve".'

'I hope he's OK.'

'No, "Steve".'

'Oh. I thought you said Steve.'

'I meant we haven't been bothered by that broadcasting guy since our sojourn in the basement at [Newspaper].'

'I see what you mean. But I've been thinking more about Steve.'

'The broadcaster?'

'No. Steve.'

After several of these frustrating circular discussions, Dida proposes that we refer to Steve as Steve and 'Steve' as fake-Steve. This is far less painful and boring. It also allows us to resume considering what the next phase of our self-appointed task ought to be. Dida refuses to treat seriously my suggestion that we move to Florida. How about Australia, my sweetheart? What say we live in my country of origin for a while?

After we solve the mystery, she says.

But Muffy would be happy there, especially after hanging around in quarantine for months.

He can be happy in Australia later.

Muffy: *I wish this television would do something. Come on. Wriggle some little points around. Put a dog in the noises. Hiss. Get shoved around the room on the wheels. Have some people shout. Go very light and then go dark again. Lazy pig.*

With all this stuff happening to me in NYC, the hat's appearance in the forest comes to seem totally out of context. I don't actually forget about the forest, probably think of it several times each day, or at least once, but at such moments the part of my mind which is responsible for declarations of 'later', 'another time', 'not now' and 'too hard' immediately clicks in.

When in New York, think not on trees.

Anyway, what I'm getting to is that with the elimination of Florida and Australia as next destinations, and the exhaustion of all other leads, demi-clues and dead-ends, we decide to return to the forest for a second search of the hat-discovery site.

This time, we need Muffy to come too. I show Muffy Steve's hat and bow tie every day, let him sniff them. I even let him carry the hat around for a few minutes, until he begins to shake it from side to side as if to stun it.

'Drop it, Muffy,' I say. Muffy stops swirling his head and looks at me.

'Put it down,' I tell him. He comes towards me and stops, just out of reach. 'Muffy . . .' Another step. I grab the hat, but Muffy doesn't let go. 'Drop it.' He lets go. 'Good boy.'

The hat retains a few tooth imprints but is otherwise undamaged. I give Muffy a biscuit and put the hat back on the cupboard. Muffy gets up on his hindlegs and scratches at the cupboard door with his forelegs as if he will eventually generate enough power to run straight up. No, Muffy, get down. Muffy sits, his head angled too cutely to describe, and gazes up at the hat longingly.

Muffy is keen, but Phil is reluctant to lend us his car again. I try to convince him through legitimate means, but do not succeed.

'I know you'll be real careful. I totally believe you. But I might need it that day,' he says. 'I have a social life outside Manhattan, same as you do.'

In the end, which is about five minutes after the beginning, I resort to dirty tactics.

'If it weren't for me, Julia would be living *not* with you, and in New England or Jersey instead of in your apartment, Phil. Just remember that for once.'

'OK, OK.' He can tell I'm going to make him give in.

We need a special permit for Muffy to enter the forest. I tell the ranger we believe we may have accidentally left potential pollutant at an old camping spot not too far from the entrance. Muffy knows the product and should find it, if it's there.

'He's a brilliant little tracker,' I explain.

The ranger looks dubious. 'That's supposed to be a bloodhound? The hell it is. I hope you find this muck, anyway. You'll be heavily fined if you go spilling oil products out here.'

'That's why I'm so concerned,' I tell him.

I give my word that Muffy will stay on a leash and will not despoil any part of the park nor chase any squirrels. I undertake to clean up after him, to indemnify the park authority against any damage he might cause or any fright he might give to other park patrons, and to report any incidents in which he becomes involved. I also agree to provide evidence that we have taken Muffy with us when we leave, and to deposit fifty dollars and Dida's driver's licence with the ranger until such evidence has been provided.

'Muffy, you now exist in the park annals,' Dida tells him at the ranger station. Muffy wags his tail and moves towards the ranger for a sniff. He doesn't get too close because the leash is only two yards long. He whines for a second, then adapts to the new situation. The ranger and Dida shakes hands. The ranger does not approach me to do the same, nor does he squat down on his haunches to take Muffy's paw. This is probably just as well as Muffy is extremely ticklish.

As soon as we're out of sight of the ranger's hut, I let Muffy off the lead. He urinates on seven neighbouring trees, and snaps at a small white butterfly. He charges down the track back towards the ranger.

'Muffy!' I hiss. He slowly returns and I slip the lead on again. Muffy is the sort of dog who gives expatriate ex-journalists a bad name. We proceed into the forest.

'It sure is nice out here,' I tell Dida. 'I could live out here for several weeks each year.'

'Mm,' says Dida. 'So could I. But not at this time of the year. In summer, yes.'

Muffy: *It's hard to believe the extreme degree to which, in some places, the city lacks density. There is so much space*

141

between buildings that a dog could run all day away from Building A and not reach Building B by nightfall. Between Building A and Building B are thousands of non-human, non-dog smells of living things, creatures which require chasing. Given the circumstances, this is impossible. The dog must traverse the emptiness between an observed starting point at Building A and the theoretical endpoint of Building B at human pace. If, by nightfall, there is insufficient evidence to support the hypothesised second building, what is the dog to do? He or she must seek to return to Building A wherein there may be sustenance or near which waits the mechanical mode of transport from the place in the city of low building density to the more regularly observed high-density district. In this, the dog appears once more to rely on human intervention in the motivation of the transport mechanism. There are no known observations of such a mechanism transporting the dog without human presence. The dog must, therefore, explain to adjacent humans the necessity of returning to the high-density district from the low-density district. Despite the setting, an explanation is achieved through the dog's conventional communicative practices.

The trees are bare now, and deep purple clouds approach from the north. The ground is muddy and a little icy. There may be snow approaching. Muffy tugs anxiously at the leash, or I think of his tugging as anxious. We are approaching the spot where Dida and I found the hat. The bare green-grey branches form a network against the purple-grey sky. Muffy whinges about his collar, stopping to scratch at it, trying to reach it with his teeth.

'Concentrate on the task at hand,' I command him. He looks at me in what would be, on a human face, a quizzical manner.

'He's OK,' Dida butts in. 'You should take the collar off of him again.'

'Not after giving that nice ranger my solemn promise. You saw what happened the first time. The little bugger ran off to dob me in,' I say. 'And who knows what poor critter Muffy may terrorise?'

On the word 'terrorise', Muffy bolts away from me to the full extent of the lead. I try to plant my right foot against the ground to stop him, but my foot lands on a frozen puddle, and slips in the opposite direction to that taken by my dog. The rest of me follows Muffy down a steep, muddy slope, and my right foot is milliseconds behind. Judging by the alternation of dark brown and grey, and assuming the former to be earth and the latter sky, I somersault three times in the course of descent. I land face first in slightly deeper mud. Muffy licks at my left hand, and at the knot of leash and fingers at its extremity.

'Are you all right?' Dida calls, and starts down after us, though with more circumspection and keeping her centre of gravity—her backside—close to the ground. I'm winded, and do not manage to reply until she is crouching beside me.

I gasp out, 'I'm fine,' so as to communicate windedness rather than broken limbs.

'How about you, Muffy?'

Muffy barks and begins to tug at the leash again.

'Muffy!' I scold. He barks and tugs. I look in the direction he's pulling. I see a pile of leaves and twigs and, underneath, some other colours: brown-red, brown-blue, and white.

'Shit,' I say. 'Bullshit.'

I push myself up, go to the heap, and crouch beside it.

'What? What is it?' asks Dida.

I pick up a stick and push some leaves to one side. Now I am sure what the coloured fibres indicate. It is the remains of a human body. I throw up.

CHAPTER 7

It is an offence not to report dead bodies. Nonetheless, after we climb up the slope away from the remains, trudge back to the ranger station, make brief polite conversation with the ranger about how we must have left our toxic waste elsewhere, drive slowly home from the forest, shower, stare helplessly around the room and at each other, try to speak about shock and disbelief, become silent, embrace tenderly for comfort and sit side by side holding hands, we do not report the dead man who was probably Steve.

I cannot completely account for this inaction, except to say that the ranger doesn't seem the right person to whom to report the body and making a report thereafter would be a much more certain decision to make, whereas we are in no immediate state to decide anything. We don't positively resolve not to report, we simply allow ourselves to skirt around it, to defer it, to promise to consider it in the near future. I suppose I believe I'll inform the police just as soon as I'm stronger, more recovered from seeing what we have seen.

Steve's body, if it was his, was a skeleton draped in rags of clothing and skin. In movies, skeletons grin demonically, sometimes with the promise of return, or with other, equally sinister promises. This body did not grin. The teeth were hidden by leaf mulch and a parchment of skin. Admittedly, this is only an impression. I was too sick to look in detail. Dida, too, covered her eyes. Ten metres below the forest path, first Dida then I burst into tears. She cried and I cried: her tears licensed—or, perhaps, brought on—mine.

I cannot remember the drive home from the forest, though it must have taken a similar number of hours to the drive out. It is dark by the time we arrive back. We go upstairs in silence. Muffy is quiet in his airline bag. There are a couple of pieces of junkmail shoved under the door; we ignore them. In its corner, the answering machine flashes that someone has called. I distractedly press PLAY. Eisie's voice booms out: 'Vernon, g'day mate. We are considering a substantial upgrade of your salary package. Please call as soon as possible.'

That night, we cannot sleep. At two in the morning, we dress, wrap ourselves in scarves and woollen gloves, and wander blearily to the supermarket. Muffy whimpers at us as we leave, but I can't face the dog-in-the-bag routine at this hour. At the supermarket, the groceries, too, are melancholy in the even, violet light. A soft drink describes itself as 'The mouthwatering flavour of natural filtered water, sugar, food acid (331), vegetable gum (414), food acid (330), natural grapefruit and peach flavours, emulsifier (polysorbate 60), preservative (211), emulsifier (480), colour (caramel).' I feel my lips pull into a pout. Why can't they group the emulsifiers? I'm going to break into tears, and the cashier will think I'm a broke junkie who's stumbled into the store by accident. Dida and I link arms and share the trolley-pushing. We choose a few products: better-quality TV dinners, dry dogfood, tea towels, flavoured Hawaiian coffees, high-cream milk. It comes to $34.85.

At home, I boil water and make coffee. In my state of mind, everything tastes too weak. I throw out the first lot and try again. Still not strong enough, but it will have to do.

I have never seen a dead body before. Dida saw her mother's; it looked as though she was sleeping angelically: 'Her face was smooth, as if death had taken away her age. Nothing like what we saw today.'

I catch sight of Dida and me, together in the mirror. We look grey. The coffee works its acidifying process on my guts. According to the thermostat, the apartment is warm, but I remain cold. I add a sweater. A while later, the outside becomes grey as well, predawn colourlessness showing up the city's damp corners. Dida and I recognise each other's symptoms as depression. Should we go get some pills? Can't be bothered. Muffy chomps noisily but without the usual enthusiasm on his dry food. At least, looking at him, I still get a momentary rush of joy. As he eats, though, melancholy returns. He is so self-contained, so much the epitome of Muffiness, that I begin to cry once more.

By noon, I think I am beginning to understand how terrorists keep going. I am beyond tired. I feel occasional nervous spasms in my limbs. I want to do something about Steve. I need to find out who murdered him and why. Dida is sleepless as well. What to do? Dida and I have trouble concentrating on each other's words. I say, 'Huh?' a lot, and Dida says, 'Repeat, I missed it,' several times. Without verbal or linguistic understanding, we nonetheless manage to generate a consensus. We come to the mumbling, circuitous agreement to confront the fake Steve.

'OK, let's go,' says Dida. I hold open the bag for Muffy, who leaps in—he no longer touches the sides—and we're away.

As we exit our apartment block, it occurs to me that sleep is what keeps my vision of New York dull. Without sleep, the city is much too bright. I'm squinting like anything and so is Dida.

'Take this for a mo',' I say, handing her the bagged dog, and return to the apartment for our sunglasses. OK, away again. Something else about sleeplessness: even the most urgent plans take longer; intervening tasks spring from everywhere. Is Muffy's collar properly adjusted? You know, Dida-honey, I could really use a stick of gum. Bus or subway? I cannot decide.

We sit in the park for a while, and Muffy chooses between pigeons. Perhaps now is the time to go to the police. It will become their problem. They'll arrest someone. I'll take the witness stand at the trial and describe how I happened to discover the body. I'll describe Muffy's discovery of the bow tie in the park, and let them draw the conclusion that Steve was kidnapped from the park and taken to the forest. There need be no connection with other charges pending against me. Just because the defence attorney will accuse me of being a foreign interloper with a long history of dishonesty and a poor work record doesn't mean my testimony will lack credibility. Just because he or she will wonder aloud how I happened to know exactly where to find the body and whose body it was, and how I happened to have personal items of the deceased's—to wit, one panama hat and one distinctive bow tie—sitting on the closet in my bedroom, would not necessarily reflect ill on my past intentions or actions toward the deceased. Just because, in the course of raising reasonable doubt, the defence attorney might narrate an alternative version in which a former-Australian ex-journalist fills the role of killer . . .

That clears that up. No police without a confession from fake-Steve.

Muffy has chosen a particularly plump pigeon, and chases it energetically each time it alights on the grass. If pigeons can feel exasperation, this one does, for it flies off. Muffy watches it go; he's as wistful as a dog can be. We head for the financial district on foot. Sleep would be too great a risk on the subway and Muffy mightn't like to stay in the bag through a bus trip. It's forty blocks but we're pumped for it. In the state beyond tired, walking and walking becomes so logical. The dog never complains.

Late afternoon, we find ourselves back in the sleazy old winebar opposite fake-Steve's office, where last time I had climbed all over the furniture installing bugging wires. The same barman chats with the same two baseball-watching, bar-leaning regulars. A large, new sign over the bar reads 'No climbing on the furniture. No dogs of any size.' I take Muffy outside, entice him into the sports bag and say loudly, 'Stay Muffy!' The barman ignores me. Dida goes to the bar and asks for cornchips and two glasses of water.

'I don't have to serve you, you know?' the barman warns her. 'I remember you.'

'I don't believe I've been here before,' Dida tells him.

'Just stay on your stools.' He gestures toward the sign. Dida gives a 'takes all types' shake of the head.

Cornchips are not as effective as amphetamines for

keeping tired people awake. This is something else I have learned in New York. An indeterminate time after the last cornchip, I sense some kind of ape—a gorilla or a thickly built orang-utan—shaking my shoulder. I'm saying to it, 'No, no, I'm a person! There are no fruits to be obtained through shaking!' I'm trying to brush off the paw but the grip's too tight and I can't move properly.

'Vern! Vern!' hisses the gorilla. I blink. The light is suddenly very dull and brown, and my face is resting in some swamp-like material.

'Oh, you've dribbled, you cute man,' says Dida. 'Come on, let's go. Our target has arrived.'

Muffy is doubly relieved to be out of the bag, wagging his tail and urinating on the winebar's welcome mat.

'That's the last time you come here,' the barman calls after us.

Halfway up in the lift, I remember we don't have a plan. What are we going to tell fake-Steve? Last time we met, Dida and I didn't even mean to confront him and we still spent days locked in a cellar. We've been warned to stay away. I think about reminding Dida of this, but it's difficult to form sentences and she doesn't look too conversational either. She looks totally wired. I feel as though the flesh at the back of my neck has been clamped, pulling the skin tight over my cheeks and jaw; it is the physical manifestation of too-tired-to-care.

The lift squeals open at fake-Steve's floor and Dida walks out, opens the broadcast-room door, walks straight through and announces to fake-Steve, 'Put your fucking hands in the air. I'm armed, angry and dangerous, and you're coming with us.'

Muffy growls. Fake-Steve raises his hands, but

doesn't say anything. He's looking around as if he has a weapon concealed somewhere or, at least, wants us to think he does. Perhaps it's less a weapon than a concealed person he's trying to conjure.

'You don't have a gun,' he tells Dida.

'Don't push me, you little prick.' She jerks her hand forward in her coat pocket. I'd believe her.

'Turn around,' she commands. 'Against the wall there. No, stay away from the desk.' (She's not falling for anything. I don't know where she gets these inspirational lines.) 'Check him, Vern.'

I've never patted anyone down before. Fake-Steve has a firm chest, a slightly softer mid-section, well-muscled thighs and buttocks, firm but not over-developed biceps and no weapons. I think about giving his testicles a little squeeze to remind him we're serious here, but he'd assume we were undercover cops. I refrain. 'He's clean,' I tell Dida, trying to maintain her shakedown tone.

'OK,' she says. 'Tie his hands and let's move.'

I cut through some wires formerly the property of AT&T, and bind his hands. I'd read that some people can expand their wrists as such moments, and relax them again later in order to effect escapes (chiefly before large crowds of admirers on television), so I tell fake-Steve, 'No flexing, now.'

'OK, OK,' he says, at last finding his role. He is clearly ready to come quietly.

As the lift descends Dida warns, 'Don't try anything smart. We've nothing to lose by hurting you.'

What a great line, Dida! Wherever did you get that one? You are a natural! I am now feeling extremely good. I understand the expression 'deliriously happy'. Exhaustion has triggered my natural opiates, I suppose.

I hail a cab and jump in, followed by fake-Steve and Dida. I tell the driver the address.

'Driver, I'm being kidnapped here,' fake-Steve rasps.

Dida laughs dismissively. I join in, though I don't get the joke.

'You horny little devil,' she purrs. 'Now don't you pay any attention to my uncle, driver. He's a very bad boy.'

The driver blushes. Dida pokes fake-Steve hard in the ribs with what might be the business end of her pistol. He gasps, but shuts up.

We arrive at our apartment block soon enough. I tip the driver, but not enough to arouse suspicion.

'Come on, "uncle",' I tell fake-Steve. I'm completely getting into this lingo. 'We're going upstairs. Cover him for a moment, Dee.'

'Right,' she replies.

'Come on, Muffy,' I say, holding open the sports bag. 'In you pop. Don't say a word,' I add to fake-Steve, whose lips have begun to twist mockingly, and who might be tempted to yell, 'He's got a little dog!' within earshot of the caretaker.

We take fake-Steve up to the apartment, sit him down, tie his legs to the chair legs and, having untied his hands, retie them to the armrests.

'Comfortable?' asks Dida, although it is obvious our guest is not, and he doesn't reply.

'OK,' she says. 'No talkies. Fair enough.'

'I've just got to get some sleep,' I say to Dida, aside.

'That's fine,' she says. 'We had to wait for them, so our impersonator here can wait a few hours too.'

I go into the bedroom. I hear Dida telling him, 'I guess you'd better start thinking about your story, feller, because if it doesn't match our information, you're in extremely big bother.'

I hear Muffy whine quietly, followed by the sound of dry dogfood poured into a dish, and Muffy's enthusiastic chewing. I fall asleep and do not dream about bodies.

Muffy: *The two great opposing impulses are the forces of settling, of rest, and those of randomness and dispersion. In New York, though, the equilibrium is between purpose and purposelessness. Humans with purpose set out from their starting points in a probably predetermined direction, attain an endpoint, which is usually marked by some length of halt, and return directly to the initial point. Humans without purpose begin in an identical manner, though they are more inclined to attain the identical endpoint through circuitous, unpredictable and indirect routings. Humans with a mix of purpose and purposelessness may either pursue their purposes circuitously or, having reached an intermediate goal, return in a leisurely, pleasurable or indirect manner. Once again, as in most of life, the dog accompanies as enforced observer.*

While the dog attempts to influence direction and pace, it often appears as though any quarter given to the dog is at the human's pleasure, and that the dog's wishes are simply co-opted into the human's decision-making process for the purposes of human pleasure. Despite this, the dog is not discouraged, and continues to make clear her or his gratificatory needs. The humans are in the process of learning that fulfilment of the dog's desires is in itself pleasure-giving. The dog's spontaneous displays of thankfulness are wondrous to behold.

The dog and the humans have stepped almost everywhere. They have stepped everywhere the dog can remember.

I wake a few hours later and Dida takes a turn sleeping. I put on the television.

'What would you like to watch?' I ask fake-Steve. 'I know you can see, so it's no use pretending.'

'I don't care,' he mumbles. 'Whatever you feel like. I've decided to capitulate completely.'

'Well, you can capitulate when my comrade wakes up,' I tell him. I am suddenly inspired. People at the centre of illegal money-making conspiracies usually feign interest in horseracing in case they ever need to account for the vast discrepancy between wage or salary and actual income. In dozens of corruption investigations and tax cases, otherwise honourable citizens make out they've won it at the races. I find horseracing on the TV.

'You like racing?' I ask, innocent-sounding.

'Not much. It's OK. I'd rather walk around, though.'

'Who do you favour in the next?' I check.

'I have no idea.'

'You're a prize bullshit artist,' I tell him. 'You really are.' But it occurs to me: the man prefers blackjack. I refrain from testing this hypothesis out. I notice fake-Steve rotating his wrists forward and back.

'I wouldn't do that if I were you,' I advise.

'What're you going to do, tell of me to your muscle?' He jerks his head towards Dida, but desists.

We watch the races. Fake-Steve appears more interested than he claims to be, though I guess his options are limited at the moment. I'm less tired than I was, and am thinking about how a nice Australian boy came to be watching US races with a vicious criminal. I'm not even sure in which US state this meet is taking place. I remember my first horserace, the excitement of the Melbourne Cup for an eight-year-old with no knowledge of horseracing. Nonetheless I had smuggled a transistor radio into the classroom. At racetime, the teacher mock-disapprovingly asked for it to be turned up. Yeah, aah, Australia. When Prime Minister Harold Holt disappeared, I was sure he'd gone on holidays. And here I am, guarding some criminal who probably believes 'holiday' is not the proper word for vacation. At least my dog has good taste. Muffy keeps growling at this guy. I cannot be sure whether my dog takes fake-Steve to be a poor-taste human being or, immobilised as our guest is, a particularly ugly-kitschy piece of furniture. Growl away, little dawg. We don't want fake-Steve to feel too comfortable here, do we?

Muffy: *Is that the scent of a cat? Is that vanillin in very small quantities? Is that a banana, or is it banana essence? Why does the waste smell so clean inside this room, when outside it is rich and thick on the nostrils? How can two spaces so close to each other smell so different? The hard-tiled room drips with ammonia and mint, the carpeted room with the bed reeks of citrus and musk, the other carpeted room overflows with the stink of alcohol and electrical circuitry and this moderately disturbing new human who makes no effort to interact. Outside, there is exhaust and salt and the mingling of human perspirations. And dogs? There are dogs aplenty. Let us gather, friends, in every clearing.*

'What a nice nap,' Dida sings loudly—and somewhat melodramatically—from the next room shortly afterwards. 'I'm going to boil a little water in the kettle, and then we can have our talk, OK?'

'I'm ready to spill beans into whatever bucket you hold out,' fake-Steve promises.

'I want to boil water,' she replies. 'Who can tell what will be spilt?'

'No need, I assure you,' says fake-Steve.

Dida has a mean streak of which I have been completely unaware. I wonder whether, given other circumstances, this characteristic might negatively impact on our relationship. So long as its object group remains sufficiently small and selective, I suppose not.

'Have appliance, will operate,' she calls as she returns from the kitchen. 'Now, sorry to keep you waiting. Are you comfortable?'

Fake-Steve says nothing. He has a problem with that particular line of inquiry. I take up position—sit in a different chair—immediately behind fake-Steve. This time I'll play the silent partner, unpredictable, menacing. And . . . away we go.

'All right, you prick,' Dida begins. 'What did you have to kill him for?'

'Kill him? Kill who?'

'See how the water's coming along there, will you sweetie?' she asks me, very, very nicely. Then continues to the prisoner: 'Don't fuck around, asshole.'

'It's just about ready,' I call. Is she serious here? Would my gentle, loving girlfriend pour boiling water on this guy? I have no idea. I decide to remain wilfully ignorant.

'Thank you!' she sings back.

'Well, yes, I guess I did hear someone had disappeared, but I had nothing to do with it. I'm not a violent person. I would have told them not to.'

'Get real,' sneers Dida. 'He was your twin brother.'

'I've been told that, but I don't know. I only know we look similar,' he weasels.

'Black tea, one sugar!' she calls, though she usually has it with cream. '*Looked* similar. Past tense. OK, Mr Co-operative. What exactly will you confess?'

I bring her the tea. She holds it menacingly, not sipping.

'Well, yes. They were moving money around and, with assistance from your friend behind me, I passed messages between them. They couldn't meet because of concerns regarding the Securities and Exchange Commission and so forth.'

'They?'

'The Editor-in-Chief and some others whose names I don't know. I don't know too much about it except that I was supposed to broadcast certain codes. That's all I was paid to do. I knew what needed broadcasting. Apparently they couldn't know. They weren't supposed to be in on the information sources. I don't think they knew which articles were significant until I broadcast the titles. Only EIC knew. It was his scam, one hundred per cent.'

'The section in which the articles appeared indicated the type of stock?'

'EIC's idea too. He organised it. By the way, *very* good.'

'Yeah, yeah. Don't brown-nose me, asshole. How did the others know which stock or commodity?'

'They must have had a decoding grid or some kind of key for each section. The placement on the page was significant, too.'

'Why the broadcast? Why didn't you meet on the Internet instead?'

'You think that wasn't considered? It's too unpredictable. The SEC's right onto that now. The National Association of Securities Dealers, too. There've already been charges laid. Not against this group, though. They've done their homework too well. They're untouchable. Can I go now?'

'No. You've got so fucking many easy answers. Name some names.'

'I don't know any. Only EIC. I think EIC is in charge of the entire operation. I followed EIC's orders. He chose the stocks to be encoded and broadcast.'

'You're lying.'

'Why should I lie? You might hurt me.'

I sit behind him as he confesses to nothing. It's not fake-Steve's fault at all, is it? It's someone else, isn't it? This guy is obviously used to police questioning. The questions continue until there is another, more implicated suspect. Just one other. Honour among thieves is not high in the corporate sector, but there's no need to give too much away.

Dida's questioning and fake-Steve's slick answers are monotonously predictable. I try to concentrate, but drift off into reminiscence. I should have written more often to old friends in Australia. I need a holiday. Australia would be so nice and warm at the moment. Mm. I smile to myself. Dida and fake-Steve talk on. There is a brief pause.

'Vern?' says Dida.

'What? Er, what?'

'We know this man's involvement is deeper, don't we? We've observed him.'

'Mm? Yeah. Er yes, we do,' I recover. I force myself to pay attention.

'What about Steve?' Dida continues to fake-Steve. 'He had nothing to do with this, did he? You murdered him for no reason.'

'I didn't even know he was dead until you told me. I had nothing to do with it.'

Dida gets up and moves to stand over fake-Steve. He looks her in the eye.

'It wasn't me. It was EIC. He told me I was a twin. I knew nothing. He must have killed him.'

'So you do know something, after all.'

'I didn't ever meet this twin. I didn't know he existed. EIC saw him somewhere and confided in him. That's all I know. I hate violence.'

'So you claim,' Dida says impatiently. 'Good-heartedness is not entirely our experience of you, but that's the way it goes. You're telling me EIC mistook Steve for you, told him too much and then got rid of him?'

'I'm saying I had nothing to do with it. It was entirely EIC. I didn't know anything about it until you just told me.'

'So you're speculating wildly, you slippery little bastard? Vern, my tea's cold. Can you boil some more water up?'

'Sure,' I say.

'I'm not speculating. EIC told me. He said, "The matter of the double has been taken care of."'

'So you know he'd killed him.'

'I assumed he'd paid him off to keep his mouth shut.'

'Bullshit.'

Fake-Steve shrugs and continues to lie. 'I'm telling you what I know.'

'Vern, a word inside?' Dida gestures towards the bedroom.

'We're going to have a go into EIC's office for evidence,' she hisses. 'What should we do with this guy? He's so horrible, and he's full of shit. I've got all this on tape, too, and I'd rather keep the tape here than him.'

'Yes. It's too distasteful to keep him in our home. He clashes.'

'Perhaps Phil will mind him?'

'Good thinking!'

I call Phil.

'Phil, we've got a little problem.'

'Drunk again? Man, you Australians really get through that beer.'

'Nothing like that. I need you to look after someone for a few hours for us.'

'A nephew or something, is it?'

'It's actually someone a little older. He doesn't mind watching TV. Can we bring him over?'

'Sure. Why not? Julia and I are home all evening. Who is he, anyway?'

'His name's fake-Steve.'

'Sounds Australian.'

'He isn't, believe me.'

'Come on buddy,' I tell fake-Steve. 'We're going next door.'

I reverse the earlier routine, this time untying him from the chair and binding his hands behind his back. We lead him to Phil's and tap on the door.

'Steve?' Phil exclaims.

'He's an impostor,' I explain. 'Don't believe a word he says. We'll tie him up in here. Whatever you do, don't untie him. He has vicious friends. He'll try to ingratiate himself. Don't listen. We'll be back for him later on.'

'Cool,' says Phil. 'It'll be a pleasure. Fuck he looks like Steve. I understand that nickname. I really do.'

'Can I say something?' fake-Steve interjects.

'No. Shut up,' I command. He shuts up. I tell Phil, 'Have fun. Thanks a lot.'

It's 9 p.m. Dida and I decide that three o'clock the next morning is the best time to visit EIC's office. New York may never sleep, but at that time parts of it become a little drowsy. We focus our minds on the office floor-plan, reminding each other of office layout, potential hiding places for incriminating papers and security guards, additional risks.

Our planning and preparation fills approximately sixteen minutes. In the movies, this wouldn't matter:

a scene is a scene, and translating a larger or smaller block of time into screen-time is unproblematic. Movie characters almost never sit around with five hours and forty-five minutes to kill. They always have specific preparatory tasks to carry out before the action moves quickly on to the mission proper. The good guys always need to pull their balaclavas down over their eyes, adjust the clips on their ski-boots, synchronise time-pieces and wish each other good luck. In the movies the only one who has to wait for anything, the only one walking anxiously to and fro, is the experienced, paternal figure. He has done it all before, but this time must wait at home or HQ for the return of the younger warriors who come of age with the inevitably successful completion of this mission.

Now, Dida and I pace around the apartment. The living room is of insufficient length for pacing. We make tea and coffee. We try eating supper but cannot become hungry even after the microwave brings the ready-to-eat boeuf bourguignon to its mouth-blistering final temperature. Dida packs a flashlight and I pack a torch. We cannot think of any other requirements.

Muffy goes through his late-night fussings about. If Dida and I were to behave like regular diurnal beings, we'd go to sleep now, and so would Muffy after he'd completed a thorough check of the premises for intruders. But no, we're irregular, always have been. Muffy lies down, yawns, gets up, sniffs at a coffee stain on the kitchen linoleum, wags his tail, picks up a formerly useful item of footwear—now a doggie toy—and pokes Dida with it, brings it over to me when Dida ignores him because she's reading a two-years-out-of-date fashion magazine, drops the toy on my shoe and wags a couple of times. Nothing satisfying occurs. He sighs and returns to his spot on the floor.

Muffy: *Life moves from the binary to the unpredictable. I look back at my antecedents and see only twos. In the future I see many things at once and only one will be true, but by then it will be looked back upon and appear binary. Two parents, four grandparents, eight great-grandparents and so on until I reach a time before dogs could measure time, when every living thing on Earth was my forebear. None-theless they were two raised to that immeasurable power. In the future I may produce any number of pups or none at all and they will look back and see the same pattern as I see now. The humans are the same, moving from their pairs in to the thronging mélange along the grey cement through the parks below. Yet humans are in a continuous state of denial, clinging to one another, clinging to the two parents, the four grandparents, remembering the past alone. They forget the millings of their sibling species, the numbers which are not two, the future which carries on and on.*

Three hours pass, mostly frittered away reading magazine rewrites of newspaper mythologies. Phil calls at midnight.

'If it's OK, we'll pick him up in the morning,' I say.

'Can I feed him?'

'Just don't poison him.'

'I'll do my best not to.'

Muffy has a barking fit a little while after. He scratches at the door, giving off little yelps of desperation.

'Shhh. You're not going anywhere,' I tell him. 'And please don't get me into any more trouble.'

A couple of hours later again, Dida and I set out for the site of our incarceration, victims returning to the scene of the crime. There are still scattered individuals and couples in the street who might stand in some kind of iconic way for crowds, but at 2.30 a.m. mean something different. They stare at Dida and me warily; I try to be vigilant. I try to be conscious of where others are standing, whether they move towards us, whether they make sudden or dangerous gestures. Everyone believes the other has wicked intentions. Why else would anyone be out at this hour? No one suspects him- or herself of essential badness. I'm clear about what I'm doing here. The city ought to issue 'I'm up to no good' placards to clarify persons too risky to make eye contact with. I've only ever seen food-stained four-year-olds wearing that slogan, on their nearly new T-shirts.

I nod to the security guard on the way into the [Newspaper] office, and flash my credit card at him. He's a mean-looking bastard, but he nods distractedly and hits the door release. Stage One accomplished: we're in. Stage Two: to find the underground office. The liftwells offer Floors 1–12 and Floors 13–29. A sign explains that access to carparks is available from all levels. Nowhere is Floor Negative 6 an option. Another security guard wanders towards the lifts. His handgun bulges in its holster. I press a button and we stare at the lights indicating approaching lifts. I've called a lift for the building's lower levels. It arrives. The guard pays no attention to us: journalists working late, probably expecting a story from Australia. As the doors close behind us I hit BASEMENT. We descend and the doors open on to the basement. I press CP; lo and behold, the carpark.

'It was definitely a personnel lift,' says Dida, in a 3 a.m. whisper. 'Wasn't it?'

'Sure,' I reply, my voice rock-solidly confident. I have no idea. We return to Floor 1 and try the upper levels' lift. Once again, we successfully arrive at the basement and carpark.

'I don't suppose you have any theories about imaginary space?' I snark at Dida.

'We'll get there. Don't worry.'

I press a couple of other buttons. The lift rises. It falls. My confidence declines.

'Try the DOWN arrow,' suggests Dida.

'Oh, sure,' I grumble. The lift drops, lights above the doors illuminating in descending order 16 15 14 13 1 B CP2 CP1. The lift runs out of numbers but continues underground. I feel a nervous thrill creep down my arms.

'This is exciting,' I whisper, gripping Dida's hand.

Dida nods, squeezing back.

The lift stops. Nothing happens. Shit. Stuck. I press DOOR OPEN. The doors open. We might be in a familiar place. There is no light, not even the reassuring red or green glow of an exit sign. We switch on our flashlights. The place is familiar. We scan the New York backdrops, our hideous and inadequate incandescent circles like mockeries of searchlights. It is too quiet in here. In another setting, this would have to be a trap: EIC's desk drawers are not locked; the filing cabinets open without a squeak. A projection for money movements for the following month lies unattended on the desk. I pick it up. The lift doors slam shut, and we hear the lift squeak through the liftwell. This could be the beginning of the end.

'Dida,' I whisper. 'You know I love you?'

'Shhh,' she breathes. She grabs my hand, and pulls me behind a backdrop. We turn off our flashlights.

'This isn't the New York I remember,' I burble.

'Vernon, for God's sake!'

We wait a few minutes. Nothing happens. We continue our search, but in total silence. In the bottom drawer are some stock certificates related to the dates of fake-Steve's broadcasts. In a filing cabinet, under 'A', we discover two air tickets to Monaco. No one has come.

We pocket the evidence and go to leave the building. Dida calls the lift. We press ourselves against the walls either side, ready to strike at a guard with our eight-inch plastic flashlights. The lift comes immediately. The doors open. No one jumps out. I peer around the corner. There is no one there, but I feel a growing sense of someone or something following us. We get in, and press 1. The lift moves smoothly up to the first floor. Not once does it stop, not once do the lift lights black out. I anticipate the firm but gentle hand on my shoulder, the sardonic smile in greeting, the relaxed aggression of still more bullyboys, trouble for Phil, a near future of lengthy imprisonment, more meetings with EIC, who will no doubt be extremely disappointed in the persistence of my attitude. Nothing happens. The doors part on Floor 1. No one is waiting for us to re-emerge. The security guard looks up as we pass. I nod at him. I'm perspiring, and am certain he will notice. He nods back. Dida keeps her head down as though shy. The security guard presses the door release again. The doors open. We step outside. If it were brighter I would be blinking, I think to myself somewhat nonsensically. A taxi passes and we flag it down.

'Probably a mistake,' I whisper. 'You should always wait for the second cab after a heist.'

We get in anyway.

'Where to?' the driver asks. We give an address a couple of blocks from home. Can't be too careful. He takes us there by the shortest route. We tip him generously.

A short walk later, we're back at our building. The whole exercise has taken little more than an hour. You sure can fill your time constructively in New York. No need to waste a minute, day or night. The new plan is that Dida and I go upstairs, retrieve fake-Steve and call the police. Surely I've now done enough that they'll overlook a couple of minor property violations: white-collar crime costs America billions every year, according to the last two-dozen generically serious magazines I've read, and we've pretty much solved a murder. I'm feeling extremely confident of having my charges dropped as we climb the stairs and see that Phil's door is slightly ajar.

'Shit,' I hiss. I tap on the door. No answer. 'You'd better wait out here in case something happens.'

This is my first act of bravery since I pulled a thorn from a lion's paw in a previous life.

I push the door open. Phil and Julia are bound to chairs with telephone wire. Phil looks up. I think he's relieved, but it's hard to tell as he has been gagged with a generous width of one of his favourite shirts.

'OK?' I ask, meaning both 'are you OK?' and 'will I continue to be OK for the next few minutes rather than getting thwacked on the head by an escaped fugitive formerly under citizen's arrest?'

They both nod. I remove their gags and set to untying them.

'The son of a bitch said he had to take a leak,' Phil said. 'I said no, but then he actually started leaking all over himself and I had a heart. Very big mistake.'

'These things happen,' I reassure him.

'Vernon, I am not apologising to you. I am recounting what happened.'

'Sure, Phil. That's OK. Don't worry. We'll get him back. How long ago did this happen?'

'About half an hour after Phil called you. Probably about twelve forty-five,' Julia answers. 'I saw the time on the video just before.'

'So that's what Muffy was on about! Is he definitely gone?' I peer into each room. Julia nods. Phil is rubbing his wrists and ankles and stretching. I call Dida in, and we lock the door.

'Did he say anything else?' I ask.

'He said, "Tell Vernon I'll write real soon." He said, "Tell him that despite everything, if he wants his old job back, there's always a place for him."'

'You're kidding? What a cheek.'

'You kidnappers sure are forgiving of each other,' Phil grumbles. 'Look at this. I've got fucking welts the size of the San Andreas fault around my wrists.'

'It's just a little chafing,' Dida tells him. 'It'll go down soon enough.'

'Thanks a lot,' he mutters. 'You go out nightclubbing or to see some arthouse film and leave us here with the gangster.'

It soon becomes apparent that Phil is losing the mood for company. We return home, first pretending to unlock Phil's door and waiting thirty seconds in case fake-Steve or his friends are in the vicinity.

Muffy is very pleased to see us, but not yet properly awake. He tries to bark but his timing is way out. His closed-mouth attempts are a passable imitation of whale song.

'Hello, you little hippy-dog,' I say, rubbing behind his ears. He manages to turn his head and lick me without biting his tongue. Then he goes back to his corner and sleeps immediately.

'Not much of a party animal,' I quip. Dida does me the favour of laughing.

Although any further action or investigation is beyond our capacity, I remain hesitant about calling the cops. I haven't had a positive experience with police since kindergarten, when one allowed me to try on his police hat. That was great. By primary school, police were already boring, entering school grounds to lecture about road safety and show poorly produced film strips. Once I'd grown into a fifteen-year-old long-hair, cops lost all pretence of good manners. I was stopped in streets throughout eastern Australia and questioned.

What's your name? What are you doing in (fill in name of town)? Do your parents know you're here? When are you leaving? What's in the bag? Just watch yourself, son. We're on to your type, believe me.

And here I am, doubly suspicious because of my accent and my allegations. On the other hand, I have to tell someone or fake-Steve will return with hordes of large men. If he is responsible for the blind man's death, I don't want him loose on the street and through the architectural publications of New York.

Dida is no help. She makes me a nice cup of tea and promises to support me in whatever decision I make. Flip a coin, Dida! Just because it started out as my mess doesn't mean you shouldn't sort it out. OK. I'll dial.

'New York City Police Department.'

'I want to report a murder and some suspicious financial transactions.'

'Which would you like to report first, sir?'

'I'd like to report both.'

'Yes sir, we can do that in time. Would you like to report the alleged homicide now?'

'I want to report both, and some other stuff as well.'

'Are those other matters related to the incident or incidents you've already mentioned, sir?'

'What difference does it make?'

'Sir, I'm simply trying to establish which alleged crime you wish to begin with.'

'I'm trying to report several at once.'

'I understand that, sir. And I'm trying to help.'

'Well, put me through to someone I can allegedly speak to, then.'

'But would you like me to put you through to our homicide or corporate law division right now, sir?'

'Oh all right. Homicide.'

'Thank you, sir. Putting you through momentarily.'

CHAPTER 8

A couple of breeders are really going for it. He's a grunter and she's a panter. The whole thing's totally percussive, with a duration of ninety seconds. Perspiration percolates to the surface of their skins. The top sheet is kicked off. Little is left to the imagination. A neatly coiffed man with salt-and-pepper hair and serious-looking metal-rimmed glasses is sitting naked on a simple wooden chair in an otherwise bare room and playing German folk melodies on a piano accordion. After ninety seconds, he stands up, bows and walks off. His replacement is a pink-lit, blue-backlit blonde woman with fantastic pelvic musculature. She flexes the triangle of her g-string towards me and exhorts me to dial 212 555 PISS. Two other big-haired women, arms coiled around one another, offer me pleasures beyond my wildest dreams.

It is 5 a.m. I have managed to report various crimes to New York authorities. I have made an appointment to meet with police officers at 8 a.m. A police officer stands outside the door of our apartment and will continue to do so until he accompanies us to the precinct office. I had stressed the danger to Dida's and my lives, and the New York authorities came through with protection. You see? They do care about us.

'I really care about you,' says another young woman in a g-string, 'and so do my beautiful friends from all around the world.'

'I will now read you a poem I have composed about love,' says a young man in a fez (Befezzed? I wonder to myself). He reads from a blue, leather-look notebook. The poem mostly rhymes. Including his introduction, the performance lasts exactly sixty seconds. After it, the young man is replaced by a middle-aged couple.

'We want to publicly declare our commitment to each other,' says the man.

'Despite some recent tribulations,' adds the woman.

Public access cable goes on and on. There are always more people ready to express.

I flick through a copy of a [Newspaper] rival. A page 9 story is headed '[Newspaper] Advertising Sales Yo-Yo Then Crash'.

Good, I think. I watch more cable. I am expressed to until it is time to leave.

At 8.02 a.m. Anna McKerry—an attorney appointed by the City to represent me—rubs her eyes and yawns as I prepare to make my statement to representatives of all concerned subdivisions of the Police Department. The police officers approach us along the linoleum corridor in pairs. They all wear serious expressions and take copious notes. Anna McKerry leans on a desk and looks bored. She, too, writes things on a pad. I promise to show the police the body in the forest and, having received assurances that nothing I assist with will be used against me in this or any other unrelated case provided I co-operate to the fullest extent of my ability, Dida and I present them with everything we've taken from EIC's office, the bow tie, tape recordings and decodings, and all the other evidence we've accumulated. Everything except Steve's panama hat, which remains on the closet at home.

'What is your involvement in this matter?' a large plainclothes policeman asks Dida.

'I'm with him,' she explains, jabbing her thumb towards me. 'He was in trouble and I wanted to help him out. Those were mean guys. They kidnapped us, you know.'

'And my little dog,' I add.

'Never mind about dogs, *Mister* Collins,' says a cop who has been tapping at a computer keyboard. 'You're due in court today. How do we know this isn't one of your tricky-foreign-thief ploys to avoid court, huh? Let's see you explain that one.'

'Shit! It's today! I'd completely forgotten. Thank you so much for reminding me.'

At this, Anna McKerry pushes herself off from the desk: a reluctant swimmer.

'I'd like a word with my client in private,' she announces. The crowd of blue uniforms moves back: the tide going out. She stage whispers, 'Why didn't you tell me about this?'

'Because we've never met before today,' I hiss back. 'You've just now been appointed to me.'

'Very funny not. Did you do whatever you've been charged with?'

'Of course not,' I harrumph. 'It's part of [Newspaper]'s harassment strategy.'

'What time are you supposed to be in court?'

'Nine-thirty, I think.'

'You think? Jesus fucking Christ. OK, I'll have to try

to get the charges dropped or postponed,' she says, loud enough for everyone in the room to have heard. She turns to the police. 'My clients will be making further statements and co-operating further in your inquiries in every possible manner. A prior matter requiring more urgent attention has intervened, however, and those statements and co-operative actions will now be delayed until at least this afternoon. Thank you, officers, and good morning.'

She makes to lead us from the room.

'Just a moment there, young lady,' says the furthest cop.

'I would prefer you not address me in that manner,' she snaps. 'It's Ms McKerry to you.'

'Excuse me, then. I must advise that if your client Collins attempts to leave this room he will be arrested. Shall we arrest your client Collins, or will you advise him to remain here?'

'I want the current charges against my client dropped immediately. What do you think you're going to arrest him for, anyway? Lack of sleep? That might be on the Jersey statute book, Sergeant, but this is New York.'

'Your client stands accused of a very serious crime and shows no inclination to permit due process to proceed.'

'My client has every intention of vigorously defending himself against these relatively trivial charges in court this morning. But in obedience to a much older law than yours, he can only be in the one place at one time. It's up to you if you want Mr Collins to continue to assist you with these far more serious crimes, or if you want him to face petty and vexatiously laid charges as he is now required to do.'

'Cool!' I whisper to Dida.

'We want these people to show us the blind man's corpse,' says the sergeant. 'Ask him who's running our case against him.'

'Who's prosecuting?' Anna McKerry asks me.

'Nicholson S. Grant's the name on the summons, if I recall correctly,' I tell her.

'It's Grant,' she repeats.

'Thank you, young lady. I heard. God, he's a total prick. Travis, tell Grant we want Collins' case postponed.'

'OK,' grunts a seated grunt.

'Now,' says my attorney, 'do you think I could meet with my clients for ten minutes? Perhaps you could search for the escaped felon in that time.'

The sergeant pulls his lips into a shape which might be meant as a wry smile, and shows us to a glassed-in booth.

Dida and I tell Anna almost everything. Anna promises to do what she can.

'Is Grant truly a total prick?' Dida asks her.

'Total.'

'He doesn't write a friendly letter,' I note.

Immediately after, Dida, Anna and I ride out to the forest in a police van with half a dozen police. I don't inform them I usually refer to these vehicles as 'pigs in a can'. I have learnt much in the last several months. At the park entrance, Dida and I stand in the door of the ranger station while the sergeant tells the ranger to close the park to visitors. The ranger glares at me.

'Where's your goddamn dog today, then?'

'You're mistaking me for someone else,' I tell him. He shakes his head.

'Fucking redneck,' he growls.

We show the cops where the body is. A uniformed cop takes photographs.

'How's it look to you, Detective?' another asks him.

'At least two shots to the head, doesn't look like suicide.'

'Mm hmm,' says the other, and writes something on a notepad. The cops mark the spot with hundreds of yards of cop-ribbon.

We drive back to the police station.

The sergeant tells Dida, 'You can go now. That's all for today.'

To me he says, 'You're also under arrest for attempting to fail to appear.'

'That's not an offence,' says Anna, horrified.

'Of course it is,' says the cop.

'I want bail right now,' she demands. 'I am very, very unhappy with you, Sergeant.'

'Police bail is set at ten thousand dollars and three times daily reporting.'

'Five hundred dollars and once a day.'

'One thousand dollars and twice.'

'One thousand dollars and once.'

'One thousand dollars, daily nine a.m. reporting, and we call him at two and eight.'

'Done.'

'You drive a mean bargain.'

'Mr Collins could turn out to be a valued client. Some do.'

The sergeant agrees to provide protection for us. We'll be driven around by police, and the apartment will be guarded, Anna explains to us.

On the way home in the cop car, Dida says, 'She seems OK, McKerry. She seems to know what she's doing.'

'She's no Harry Pewley,' I say. 'But yes, I have to agree.'

We take the lift up with our assigned protector, who insists on entering the apartment first.

'OK,' he calls. 'All clear.'

In our absence, the apartment has been 'searched'— that is, ransacked. All the drawers are pulled open, clothing is everywhere, the bed has been overturned. The borrowed computer equipment is gone. The borrowed desk on which the borrowed computer equipment used to sit: it's gone, too. Not a good sign for my theft case.

'Protection, eh?' I ask the cop.

'Standard procedure, nothing to do with me,' he mumbles.

Dida and I clean up. I notice Steve's hat remains, undisturbed, on top of the closet.

Over the next few days, Dida and I meet often with the chief prosecuting attorney, a large, morose ex-detective named Stanley Stoneman. My theory is that Stanley's mood would be much improved by TV fame. Dida believes he needed the fame at a much younger age and that Stanley will always be morose into the future.

Each day Stanley and I repeat this conversation:

'I'm particularly co-operative, aren't I?'

'You appear to answer my questions.'

'If not for me, your case would be significantly weaker, wouldn't it?'

'That depends if we get a conviction.'

'I hope you're noting the extent of my co-operation with you. Are you noting it?'

'There is little that passes me.'

During our second meeting with Stoneman, we watch EIC being led in, cuffed and unshaven.

We hear the sergeant read the charges: murder, kidnapping, fraud, felonious breaches of fiduciary duty, breaches of various stock-trading provisions, theft.

'Good,' I say.

'Fuck yeah,' agrees Dida. 'He's going to the big house for a long time, I hope.'

EIC says nothing. A slick-looking lawyer arrives and accuses the sergeant of 'harassing a perfectly respectable citizen'. The police 'clearly have the wrong man'. The superintendent will not be pleased at the embarrassment to his precinct, will he? The party moves into the glass booth. When Dida and I leave, the young attorney is still gesticulating at police.

My bail conditions do not preclude walks with Muffy, whose mood seems unaffected by the chaos around.

Muffy: *New York is the last of the real cities, the last of the cities built of stone. Chimeras guard the stone buildings, staring down the sheer sides at the loiterers in the streets. Inside, electronic eyes blink on . . . and off . . . and on . . . languid, sleepy, bloated with video morality.*

Satyr cast in bronze, staring east
Two-headed sea-monster attacking a whale
Vulture with three eyes—one pineal (probably
*   blasphemous)*
Creature with organs on the outside
Giant antelope of silver with two sets of human genitalia
Thing which is person by night, invisible by day
Giraffe with lightbulb for head
Goat-dog with bared teeth and oxide saliva
Centaur bearing a drawn bow
Many-eyed woman pushing forward from the rooftop
Papier-mâché beetle ten metres long.
Insects explode in purple electric traps. The day expires.

A week later, Dida and I have told Stanley about

the history of my employment by [Newspaper], the disappearance of Steve and the appearance of fake-Steve, the terrible trauma of our kidnapping by Eisie and fake-Steve, the broadcast set-up, the discovery of the body, and our personal heroics in making our citizens' arrest of fake-Steve. I freely employ the phrase 'apparently at the behest of EIC'.

We describe the hidden sub-basement office in the [Newspaper] building and our cleverness and noble intentions in searching it for incriminating material. We attempt to shudder visibly at the recollection of harassing answering-machine messages and nasty letters. We are incredibly helpful to these poor plodders who have no idea what really happens in a newspaper office.

'If not for us, there would be no case,' I explain.

'Not much of a case anyway,' complains Stanley. 'We can't find the missing twin and everyone else is blaming him for everything.'

'But EIC's your main man,' says Dida.

'Not according to his version. He thinks he's a lackey.'

'Whose lackey?' I ask.

'The usual Mr Big type: the unseen brains behind the outfit who plans each crime and takes all the profits. Do you know who that might be?'

'Major shareholders,' I guess.

'Wow,' ironises Stanley. 'No wonder you rose through the ranks of journalism so quickly. Could you be less specific?'

I list a few famous shareholders.

'Nope,' says Stanley. 'No. Not that one. Uh-uh. Nuh.'

'OK, wise guy, who then?' says Dida defensively.

'Think about it,' says Stanley. 'I'll see you tomorrow.'

Police protection now means they give tokens for the busfare if no one feels like driving us. No one ever feels like driving us. The desk sergeant tells us today's tokens are the last. We catch the bus home.

Stanley's mood has affected the entire city. We are forced witnesses to the painful interactions for which mass transit systems are perfectly designed. A couple behind us argue about whose turn it is to take the cat to the veterinarian. An elderly woman tells the driver, 'I paid already. You saw me put the token in,' while the driver shakes her head.

Compensation: as always, Muffy is waiting. I take him for a long, slow walk. It is very cold, but Muffy doesn't mind at all. As we walk, I imagine I know how Winston Smith feels at the end of 1984, exhausted enough to love the enemy. It's all too much, I whisper to myself. I know I should be affirming: 'Yes, Vernon, you have made it through.' But I'm not, I'm miserable. I spend my days talking to cops and lawyers. My former career has been exposed as a front for villains and murderers. The future promises: litigation.

How would an American deal with this? Hell, I dunno. When I attend a baseball game at O'Shea Stadium, its stands packed with enthusiastic Americans, I'm the one guy there—the one in tens of thousands—who doesn't know the words to the national song. Imagine that, all these Americans defined only in relation to me, and there I am, relatively Australian. It's not possible to be Australian in any other way, I suppose.

All the next moves are for American cops and lawyers to make. They'll haul me before the courts as the accused and the witness. They'll sneer at me and defend me. They'll show computers in clear plastic bags to the judge and they'll ask me to identify my kidnappers. Face it, Vern, life is out of your control.

That night, this is my dream: When Dida won't come to me, I curl up inside. I tighten my calves, I clench my jaw, I hurl stones at the sun. I smash bottles in the street, I pick the paint off fences, I swear uncontrollably at doctors, I clap my hands to scare the pigeons, I switch on all the lights, I drink until I fall, I give up my guts for her, I cry myself to sleep. I wake up and Dida is there saying, 'What? What? Oh, a dream.'

Each day, Dida buys [Newspaper]. There is no report of the charges against any member .of its executive. Other papers have trumpeted every development. One even carries a fuzzy page 2 pic of Muffy and me. Muffy's head protrudes from a sports bag. The caption reads: 'Vernon Collins: assisting police'. [Newspaper] boasts of increased sales. A competitor notes, '[Newspaper] boasts of increased sales, but advertisers are turning off in droves. According to Mr Klim T of advertising agency Xavier & T, advertisers do not like [Newspaper]'s editorial move downmarket.'

[Newspaper] replaces its front-page human interest stories with daily page A-1 startling news: 'Fragment of Commandment Found at Mt Sinai: Archaeologist'.

'Don't buy it any more,' I beg Dida. 'I can't stand it.'

'One more week,' she says. 'They can't maintain this silence.'

'Watch them.'

A week later, [Newspaper] carries a story on testing the efficacy of New York's electric chair using saline-filled heavy-duty balloons joined together to resemble the human form. Next to this is a head-and-shoulders photograph of me—my by-line photo, but much enlarged. The headline is 'Charged [Newspaper] Sub-Editor "Thief and Con-Artist".' Of course, [Newspaper] still hasn't confessed to its own wrongs.

'You see?' I say.

'I do,' says Dida.

Anna McKerry calls.

'You're going to trial next week,' she tells me. 'Unless you have another attorney, I will represent you.'

'Thank you. I'll stick with you.'

'Regarding the proceedings against you, meet me this afternoon, please, three p.m. sharp.'

'Fine.'

'One other thing.'

'Mm.'

'If there's anything the police know about you that I don't, it would be better if I knew it too.'

'Why should there be?'

'Your former boss has bail conditions far less strenuous than yours.'

'Bail? For kidnapping and murder? They used to be serious offences.'

I am shocked. EIC's on the loose again.

'So think about what else you need to tell me,' she finishes. Click.

'Fuckfuckfuckfuckfuckfuckfuckfuckfuckfuckfuck fuckfuckfuckfuckfuckfuckfuckfuckfuckfuckfuckfuck fuckfuck.'

'What?' says Dida, grasping my sleeve. 'What's happened? What? What?'

'Fucking EIC's got easier bail than I fucking have. And I'm going to fucking trial next week.'

'That complete asshole,' comforts Dida.

About five minutes later, Eisie calls.

'What?' I say.

'Hi, Vern. I wondered if we could do a little deal.'

'No deals.'

'I'm facing a couple of minor misdemeanour charges, and I was hoping you'd be a character witness for me.'

'You're fucking kidding.'

'I'm accused of helping cover up some teeny little financial agreements that seem not to be quite straight. I really had no idea. I was sure they were OK. You know I wouldn't knowingly break a law, and I know the same about you, so what do you say? Can we trade statements?'

'Fuck off.'

'It's a pity, Vernon. I still think of you as my friend.'

'Goodbye, Eisie.'

'See you later. Good luck in your trial. I'm glad the charges against me aren't as serious as the ones you face.'

I guess Ma Bell's offering discounted phone calls today. Within half an hour there's another too-familiar voice at the other end: EIC.

'Hello Vern. Long time no see.'

'It's you,' I say, redundantly.

'I think we should reconcile.'

'I'm reconciled to you being an asshole and my career not existing.'

Dida nods supportively from across the room. Muffy begins to growl. In times of trouble, you can always rely on family.

'Come on, Vernon,' slimes EIC. 'We're really on the same side. We have both been wronged by that dirty, conniving murderer. We ought to support each other. Perhaps we can make a difference. Perhaps we can

help convict that man. He's tricked both of us, you
know.'

'He didn't trick me. We were on to him from the
moment the eyes appeared in his head. And if that's
your story, you ought to change it to something more
closely resembling your personal experience.'

'You've always been sharp, Vernon. That's why
you're so invaluable to us at [Newspaper]. Which is
the second reason I've called. Vernon, why don't you
return to work, and we'll sort out the little matter of
you pinching our computers so no harm's done.'

'I'm not interested.'

'Think on it.'

'No.'

'Look, Vernon, I'm sorry that magazine went to you.
New York appears to be a big city, but really it's no
bigger than Petrol Pump, Alabama. It's a damn shame
the magazine got you into so much trouble.'

'Sure, pal,' I say bitterly. 'I totally believe you. But
don't call me again.'

'You be in touch when you're ready,' he says firmly,
or commands gently.

'No,' I repeat, and hang up on him.

It's a small victory to me. No one ever hangs up on
editors. People are usually too desperate to suck up
to them. Yet I know better than to feel too triumphant.
As I tell Dida, 'Tiny wins are the building blocks of
humiliation and overall defeat.'

'Oh, Vern,' she says. 'It'll be OK.'

We embrace and, following on, obtain considerable
sexual comfort from each other.

'Bad luck about EIC, too,' Anna greets me that afternoon.

'Why? What's happened?' I start. 'Is he dead?'

'No, he'll probably give himself a raise. Serious plea bargaining. The S.O.B. won't even serve time. Pleads guilty to knowingly concealing an offence. That's all. I don't think the police tried for anything more.'

'Kidding?'

'I'm not kidding: I'm a lawyer. EIC blamed fake-Steve for everything. Claimed fake-Steve was Mr Big after all. The Ds believe him, or believe him enough for now. Or have been convinced through non-legal means.'

'Fake-Steve was Mr Big! What about Eisie S~?'

'He's gone over to the police as a witness against fake-Steve. All charges have been dropped.'

'Fuuuuuuuuuuuuck!' I yell.

'Very good,' says Anna. 'I want you to build on that feeling, but try it without the swearing. I think you've been under a lot of pressure. If you can maintain it through the court case we can plead seriously mitigating mood swings. We can try to have the big charge reduced and the others dropped or incorporated into the theft.'

'But I'm innocent,' I protest. 'You're supposed to be my attorney. You're paid by the government to believe me.'

'I believe you. Of course I do. I believe all my clients,' she says. 'But you must understand that Law is ninety-five per cent pragmatics and five per cent corruption, and the other side has snapped up that five per cent.'

'I'm not giving [Newspaper] the satisfaction.'

'It's your call,' she says, resignedly. 'But you'll have to face all the listed charges.'

'I'll face them.'

No charges are laid against members of * cartel, either. An SEC enquiry found 'no evidence of markets

tampering or other acts in breach of any laws govern-
ing corporate behaviour'. This despite Dida's tape of
fake-Steve's confession. The day before my trial, I
catch a glimpse of a report in [Newspaper]'s business
section: 'New Symbol on Wall Street'. There is a photo
of a grey-suited businessman in front of a large backdrop. I do not recognise the businessman, but the
backdrop is pained with a large *. The cartel has gone
public.

My own court case goes as well as can be expected.
Unlike the Red Queen, the judge agrees that the trial
should precede the sentence. He follows US law to the
best of his ability. He goes along with our proposition
that evidence be presented by both the prosecution *and*
the defence. The prosecution tenders video evidence
of me loading bags up with computer equipment.
They call [Newspaper]'s property manager as their
only witness. He makes the case that the equipment I
am videoed taking is [Newspaper]'s. The equipment
itself sits in a corner of the courtroom. Anna doesn't
bother to cross-examine.

'Call Vernon Collins,' calls the court clerk.

'Yep,' I answer, as though answering at eighth grade
roll-call.

'This is a case of an honest mistake on my part being
maliciously misconstrued by my former employers,' I
tell the court. 'Of course I had various items of [News-
paper]'s computer equipment in my apartment. I
freely admit that. I admit that both the hard drive and
the monitor were engraved with [Newspaper]'s security marks. I concede that I was not free to hold on
to that equipment once my employment had been terminated. In all these matters, I am one hundred per
cent with the prosecution case.'

'And?' asks Anna, pausing between paces across the width of the courtroom.

'And in contemporary American employment, it is very difficult to know when one's employment has been terminated. I totally believed—and still honestly do—that I am an employed person. Sure my editors don't send me as much work as they used to, but I did some work a month or so ago, and some more work a while before that. But I've also been working for other companies, through a freelancers' agency. [Newspaper] has never liked this. They want sole rights to my work and skills without responsibility for my well-being, for ensuring a decent and ergonomic working environment, for providing a structured career path. I'm still a young man, and I need to think about my future. This action, as far as I'm concerned, is not about stealing at all. It's about whether a free citizen ought to be able to sell his labour freely.'

By the end, Anna McKerry has tears in her eyes. Dida, who's sitting at the back of the court, is nodding in the manner of people expressing solidarity. The prosecutor looks a little despondent. Even I am believing myself.

'Well done,' whispers Anna as I return to my chair.

The judge retires for about a minute, then returns.

'I find you guilty as charged,' he pronounces, 'and sentence you to two years' imprisonment. Owing to your prior good record and impassioned belief in freedom of the individual, I have decided to suspend that sentence for the moment. I order that you lodge a bond of two thousand dollars and be of good behaviour for three years. Any more trouble and you're in the clink immediately. Do you understand the second chance I am giving you?'

'Yes, Judge, I do,' I breathe.

'Get out of my court.'

'Thank you.'

'Whoo-hoo!' I whoop, once we're outside. 'Thank you, Anna. It was a pleasure to work with you.'

We shake hands.

Dida and I walk home through the snow, arm in arm. I am thinking about our nice, warm bed in our nice, warm bedroom. I do not ask Dida what she is thinking. I permit myself to assume we are in perfect accord.

At the apartment block, we arrive as Phil and Julia carry suitcases downstairs.

'We're moving out,' Julia tells us. 'I've got a job in Annapolis, Maryland. Your vicious friend was the last straw for us and New York. Nice to know you, though. Goodbye.'

We shake hands. I hug Phil.

'I'll write to you, you old bastard,' I tell him.

'Bullshit,' says Phil.

I laugh. He doesn't.

Muffy greets us at the door. I'm sure he senses my new lightness. I notice he is holding a piece of coloured cardboard in his mouth.

'Drop it,' I tell him. He wags his stubby little tail and ignores me.

'Muffy,' I scold. He approaches warily.

Muffy: *Any dog knows that life is perfectible. The dog passes through the infinite poses between step and step and senses which position is the right one. She or he keeps moving, preserving these movements in memory. In running through the park, there is one faultless place. In scratching maniacally at the door, only one paw-stroke is the ideal. In negotiating the possession of an object . . . A dog knows these things, and nothing more need be said.*

I snatch the postcard, and Muffy relinquishes it. The scene is a generic beachfront, built up with international-style hotels. It bears the superscription 'Monaco' in gold italics. Muffy wags his tail to encourage me to throw the postcard back to him. Instead, I turn it over to read. There are no words other than our neatly handwritten address. The only other mark is a symbol: *. This man whose birth record is blank has erased himself from America again. In another country, fake-Steve is having a good time. I flick the postcard to Muffy, who snaps it from the air and shreds it enthusiastically.

I cannot tell if one day I too will travel again, if I will return to Australia. As we undress, Dida tells me it is not unimaginable. I'm not so sure. Perhaps the logic of my life will permit the crossing of an ocean, but that is not enough. I do not know that it is possible to return, that I retain enough of my old self so that my arrival in Sydney would be a return and not a fresh journey. Australia, if there ever were such a complete place to occupy, might have closed over on my departure more than a decade before. Small ripples across the surface of a lake and then stillness.

I take the blind man's hat from the top of the cupboard. This early winter afternoon is cold and clear. I open the bedroom window and fling the hat out. Instead of falling brim over peak the several storeys down to the street, an updraft must catch it. The hat spins away at eye level, like an old LP, between the rows of Manhattan apartment buildings, around a corner and out of sight.

CREDITS

Publisher: Sophie Cunningham

Inhouse editor: Annette Barlow

Production manager: Lou Playfair

Editor: Sandy Webster

Proofreader: Sandy Webster

Publicist: April Murdoch

Cover designer: De Luxe & Associates

Typesetter: **DOCU**PRO

Printer: Australian Print Group